**"The tension you refer to is real enough."**

Leon leaned against the door, smiling humorlessly. "It's physical. Sexual, if you like. I don't think I need to say any more—you know what the remedy is."

Cherry's heart was pounding with alarm. "You—you don't mince your words, do you?"

"Listen to me—" his face was impassive "—and remember what I tell you. David is dead. You are alive and a young and very desirable woman. You also want me as much as I want you. It's inevitable that we'll become lovers. You need time, and I'll give it to you. But believe me, when I decide to make love to you, you won't have any say in the matter!"

# Books by Claudia Jameson

## HARLEQUIN PRESENTS

## HARLEQUIN ROMANCE

These books may be available at your local bookseller.

Don't miss any of our special offers. Write to us at the following address for information on our newest releases.

Harlequin Reader Service
P.O. Box 52040, Phoenix, AZ   85072-2040
Canadian address: P.O. Box 2800, Postal Station A,
5170 Yonge St., Willowdale, Ont.  M2N 6J3

# CLAUDIA JAMESON

## the scorpio man

**Harlequin Books**

TORONTO • NEW YORK • LONDON
AMSTERDAM • PARIS • SYDNEY • HAMBURG
STOCKHOLM • ATHENS • TOKYO • MILAN

Harlequin Presents first edition September 1985
ISBN 0-373-10817-6

Original hardcover edition published in 1984
by Mills & Boon Limited

# CHAPTER ONE

'MRS SIMSON, if you'll follow me, Mr Moore will see you now . . .'

Cherry Simson got to her feet, unperturbed by the interview which was about to take place. She had met Alec Moore several times during the past three years and she'd always found him pleasant. Besides, why should she be nervous when she really didn't care whether she got this job or not?

The woman from Personnel smiled as Cherry stepped into the carpeted lift, on the back wall of which was a floor to ceiling mirror, slightly tinted. The Head Offices of Silver & Silver Limited were certainly smart.

Although she had worked for the company for three years, Cherry had never actually been here before. Situated in the West End of London, the Head Offices occupied a building comprising five floors of luxuriously appointed suites. The carefully tended plants in the corridors, the plush carpeting and immaculate decor did not impress her, because it was only what she had expected. Silver & Silver Limited was a well-established company which had kept up with the times and grown steadily during years of trading which spanned almost a century.

The company's business was that of designing, manufacturing and installing air-conditioning systems both at home and abroad. During the past ten years in particular its expansion had been rapid, years during which it had been under the managing directorship of Leon Silver, a man Cherry had never met.

'You've met Mr Moore, of course?' The woman from Personnel gave her a reassuring smile as the lift doors

5

opened on the fifth floor, where the directors' offices were, presumably.

'Several times, briefly, on his visits to my boss at the regional office in Bristol.' Cherry's hand went automatically to touch the near-black hair which she had swept into a softly styled chignon. Stray wisps of curls framed a face with a pale but flawless complexion. She had dressed for this interview as she dressed for every ordinary working day, with smart simplicity.

Uncaring though she was about the outcome of the interview, her beautiful eyes, eyes of a very unusual hue, were busily absorbing everything around her. She followed the woman down a corridor carpeted in dark green, on the walls of which were huge photographs of equipment and of Silver & Silver's factory and sheet metal works in Southampton.

They stopped at a door marked 'Alec Moore, Sales Director' and found themselves not in his office but in that of his secretary, a girl of similar age to Cherry, an extremely pretty auburn-haired girl with a friendly smile. 'Good morning. I'm Karen Black, Mr Moore's secretary. He's on an overseas phone call at the moment—please sit down.'

'Thank you.'

'I'll leave you to it then.' The woman from Personnel handed a folder to Karen and then retreated, having completed her job by escorting Cherry to the directors' offices. 'Good luck, Mrs Simson.'

'Thank you,' Cherry said again, this time to her well-wisher. The half-hour she had spent with the personnel manager had gone well, and if her interview with Alec Moore was similarly successful, maybe she would soon be taking over from his present secretary.

But did she want to, really? Did she want to be secretary to the Sales Director of the company? Did she want to work here, at Head Office, when it would necessitate her moving to London?

Her parents wanted this for her, there was no doubt

about that. She sighed inwardly, a little sigh of resignation. She was here as much for her parents' sake as her own. More, in fact. Much as they loved her, they wanted her not only to leave home but also to leave Bristol, the city in which she had lived all her life.

'It's been three years, Cherry...' The words had come from her mother during breakfast about a month earlier. They were the opening words of a little speech which was becoming predictable to Cherry, except, of course, that last year it had begun with, 'It's been two years...'

'Over three years, actually. Cherry, don't you think it's time you made some changes in your life, in your routine? I'm not suggesting anything drastic but, well, you don't want to live with us for the rest of your life, do you?'

Cherry had looked at her father then, wanting to know how he felt. 'Your mother's right,' he said gently, his eyes full of concern. 'I—we both feel it would be a good idea for you to leave home, to leave Bristol, in fact. There are too many memories here, painful memories, and this isn't helping you to—well, as your mother says, it's been more than three years since David died and you're still not...'

Over it. Cherry had finished her father's sentence silently. How many years did it take to get over the death of one's husband? Would she *ever* get over it? Would she ever adjust to life without David, become the happy, smiling girl she used to be?

No. Never. The change which had taken place in her life three years ago was irreversible. The change in her, irrevocable. But she couldn't say that to her parents, they worried about her enough as it was.

Only a few days after their pep-talk, she had seen the job at Head Office advertised in Silver & Silver's company newsletter and she'd decided to apply for it, mainly because it would please her parents. Their concern for her, unfounded though it was, had in turn started to worry her and she had forced herself to take positive action for their benefit. She had always got on well with her parents, whom she loved dearly, and she didn't particularly want to leave home. Nor did they want to get rid of her; they just thought it would be best for her. After David's death, they had given her total, unfaltering support ... but they clearly felt it was now time she stood on her own two feet, that after three years she should be equipped, emotionally, to do that.

Emotionally. What sort of state was she in emotionally? What, exactly? Her eyes moved unseeingly around Karen Black's office as she thought about that.

Stable. Very stable, because in truth there was very little which stirred her emotions. Whether she was living in Bristol or in London wouldn't make much difference to her, actually. Her routine wouldn't change because she was perfectly happy with it as it was. And it wasn't far from London to Bristol; she could drive home at the week-ends.

Of course there was nothing to say she'd get this job. Having three years experience as secretary to the manager of a regional sales office did not necessarily mean she was suitable for a high-powered position as secretary to the Sales Director. And it was from these prestigious offices that the international business was conducted. How much of her experience of regional office business would come in useful here?

Her eyes focused and registered what she was seeing and she looked around the office with a little more interest. 'This seems like a nice place to work—light, airy offices and all the latest equipment, by the look of things. And I imagine——'

'Oh, it is!' Karen Black's enthusiasm was obvious. 'But I'll tell you this much ...' She put paper into her typewriter and carried on working as she talked. 'If you get this job, you'll work hard, and I mean hard. But there are lots of perks. We have our own dining rooms here and subsidised lunches which are extremely good.

That's worth a lot, don't you think?' She smiled, not waiting for an answer. 'I live alone and so I hardly ever bother to cook a meal in the evenings. There's no need! I have a substantial meal here. And there's all the fresh coffee you can drink, five weeks paid holiday and——' She broke off, laughing at herself. 'But there's no need for me to tell you what a good company this is to work for, you know that much already! Which region are you from?'

'Bristol. Still, things are bound to be different at Head Office . . .'

Karen's attention shifted to the small switchboard on her desk. 'He's finished his call. Hang on, I'll tell him you're here.' She got to her feet and moved to an adjoining door.

'Are you——'

The other girl stopped and turned to look at Cherry, whose voice had grown just a bit taut. 'Sorry, it's—I just wondered why you're giving up the job?' Her eyes went to the door of Mr Moore's office.

Karen laughed softly. 'No, it has nothing whatever to do with Alec. Believe me, he's the ideal boss, a really super man to work with. With, you see? I've always felt that I work with him rather than for him.' She grinned, lowering her voice as she jerked her thumb in the direction of another adjoining door. 'I doubt whether Anne would say the same things about her boss! Not at the moment, anyhow!'

'Anne?'

Karen's voice went even quieter. 'Anne Mellor. She's secretary to our MD and Chairman . . .'

Who were one and the same person. Leon Silver. He had succeeded his father as Chairman a year ago, having been MD for nine years prior to that.

Cherry's eyebrows went up slightly. 'I've never met Mr Silver.'

'A hard task master! But then the man at the helm needs to be, don't you think? In my opinion he's A-okay, and Anne thinks very highly of him, really. It's just that she's a bit sour at the moment because she's just discovered she's pregnant—and Mr Silver is hopping mad about it. He doesn't want to lose her, you see, and Anne's told him she'll leave when the baby's almost due. No maternity leave for her. She and her husband have been trying for a family for years and she's got no intention of working after the baby's born.'

Cherry nodded. She wanted to say it was selfish of Leon Silver to resent losing his secretary when it was for such a nice reason, but integrity prevented her.

Her voice returning to its normal volume, Karen went on. 'I got sidetracked, didn't I? You were wondering why *I'm* leaving.' She shrugged philosophically. 'It's no secret that I don't want to leave here. But I've just got engaged,' she explained, waving her left hand in the air. 'I've worked in England, here, for almost six years—and what's happened? I've met a New Zealander! I've met someone who lives about a hundred miles from my home in Auckland! Small world, isn't it?'

Cherry smiled. She hadn't realised Karen was from New Zealand; she had no detectable accent. 'So you're going home to New Zealand to get married.'

'I'm going home to get married and to settle,' came the smiling amendment.

She walked into her boss's office, taking with her the personnel papers concerning Cherry, and two minutes later Cherry was shaking hands with Alec Moore.

'Mrs Simson, it's good to see you again! You're well, I take it? And how's Bob? . . . Please sit down.'

Cherry sat, answering the question about her boss in Bristol. 'Bob's fine, thanks. He sends his regards.'

'I must say, I was surprised that you applied for this job,' Mr Moore went on, his eyes sweeping over her impassively as he settled in the plush leather chair behind his desk. 'Very surprised.'

With eyes which were far from impassive, Cherry looked at him. His remark interested her, disturbed her.

'But why? I've had three years experience with the company and——'

Mr Moore dismissed that with a wave of a hand. 'Oh, yes, yes. I know that. I don't doubt for one moment that you're well qualified and capable of taking over from Karen.' He smiled, an open, full-blooded smile which added to his good looks. 'Needless to say, Bob Langley has put in a good word for you—even though he hates the idea of losing you to Head Office!'

That was gratifying. But it didn't answer Cherry's question. 'So why the surprise, Mr Moore?'

He hesitated before answering, watching her. 'I wrote the ad. in the company magazine myself and I specifically said that applicants must have no ties, must be free to travel at short notice——'

'Yes?'

'Well,' he shrugged, 'I don't regard you as a person with no ties. I mean, surely your husband won't like the idea of your taking off——'

'But Mr Moore, I'm a widow.' The words came quickly and painlessly. It no longer upset her to refer to herself as a widow, nor did the subject of David upset her, though she never talked about him to strangers.

The man on the other side of the desk just blinked. Obviously he was as astonished by the information as Cherry was that it was news to him. Dropping his eyes to the desk, he said, 'I'm sorry. Bob never mentioned that. I'd always assumed . . .' It was only then that he opened the folder which had been put together by the personnel manager.

Cherry leaned back in her chair and relaxed. Of course Mr Moore had assumed she had a husband; at the age of twenty-four she was an unlikely candidate for widowhood. On the occasions when he visited the regional office managers, he had more important things to talk about than the marital status of young secretaries who wore wedding rings. And there was no reason on earth why Bob Langley should have volunteered this information.

'Your assumption was the natural one,' she said. 'But as you'll see, I have no ties, no commitments.'

'And you'd be prepared to travel with me when necessary?'

'Certainly.' She was glad he'd phrased his question so. If he'd asked her whether the idea of travelling appealed to her, she couldn't in honesty have said yes. On the other hand, it wasn't an unappealing prospect either.

Enthusiasm. That's what she lacked, over this and virtually everything else in life. Oh, how the Cherry of a mere few years ago would have loved the idea of travelling! She closed her eyes briefly. What a stupid thought. The Cherry of yesteryear wouldn't have been able to apply for a job which involved travel, because that girl had a commitment—to her husband. A binding, total commitment she had been only too willing to make . . .

Alec Moore was taking his time, doing a thorough job of reading every word on the papers in front of him. Cherry waited quietly, ready for the questions which would inevitably follow, weighing him up in the meantime.

He was a good-looking man who appeared to be in his early forties. His straight hair was the colour of sand and there was plenty of it. His light brown eyes were probably his nicest feature; they were honest, open, but she didn't for one moment forget that there must be a tough streak in her hard-working prospective boss. And a determined streak. Nobody got to the position of Director with a company such as this without those qualities.

Cherry had always found him pleasant. Now she decided she liked him. A little enthusiasm stirred within her, just a little.

There were no questions from Mr Moore, not for the time being, anyhow. He did the talking. He gave her a fifteen-minute description of what her duties would be, of basic details concerning the sales he was mainly involved with.

As he talked, Alec Moore watched Cherry with eyes which were deceptively shrewd. His fingers fiddled with a pencil, his mind taking note of the impressions she was making on him as he gave her cursory details of what she could expect if she became his secretary.

She was, he saw from her eyes, interested but not enthusiastic. There was also a good deal of intelligence in her eyes—which were a pleasure to look at. Hell, how did one describe those big, gorgeous eyes, exactly? Violet. They really were violet! They'd been the first thing he'd noticed about this girl at the time he had first met her. The second thing had been her smile. That was stunning. It almost made you feel as though you'd been rewarded for something when she smiled at you.

But she wasn't smiling now. She hadn't smiled since she'd walked into his office. A twenty-four-year-old widow, eh? He wouldn't ask her about that. It was none of his damned business, it wasn't relevant so he had no right to ask about it.

He was as yet unsure about her as a prospective secretary, but one thing was certain: she would be a delight to look at, a pleasure to have around. He appreciated having a pretty face around and this girl was more than pretty, she was ... Still—he sat erect now, leaning forward slightly, elbows on desk—he needed someone who was much more than an ornament. He must not be influenced in any way by beautiful, intelligent eyes which did their utmost to hide a sadness he'd never noticed in them before. What would Leon make of her? he wondered. Leon Silver was the best judge of character he'd ever encountered, which was quite a compliment coming from Alec, himself an extremely good judge of people—usually.

He stopped talking and waited, keen, interested to see how she would respond.

When Mr Moore finished speaking, Cherry paused for a moment to make sure he'd done before she started to ask questions and make comments. She had dozens of them. At some point during the past few minutes she had made up her mind that she wanted this job after all. She thought fleetingly of her parents, who had driven her to London this morning and would be meeting her for lunch in a nearby restaurant. They had done her a favour by taking her to see the house in Hampstead *before* her interview. It meant that she was able, now, to exclude from her thinking any worry over finding suitable accommodation in London. How clever they were! It had been no accident, the way her father had organised this day!

'Mrs Simson, I'm a busy man and I think at this stage it would be a good idea for you to tell me whether you're still interested in the job before we go any further. Well?'

Cherry looked at him in surprise, taken aback by his question, his tone. 'Yes, of course I am! Very much so.' And so she was, far more than she'd expected to be. Alec Moore had not attempted to sell the job to her, he'd known better than to do that, but while listening to him Cherry had realised what a real challenge it would be, working for him—with him. He had a lot of responsibility on his shoulders, some of which would in turn be passed on to her, and she would welcome it. For the first time in a long time, she saw before her a goal, something to prove—mainly to herself.

'Then perhaps you'll start by telling me why you applied for the job, why you're prepared to move to another city?'

She pulled herself together smartly. This was make or break for her, and he must have interviewed other applicants, or have more to see. Silver & Silver always put their vacancies in their newsletter first, before advertising elsewhere, and she wouldn't be the only person to have applied from one of the regions.

Smiling warmly at him, fired with confidence now, and inspiration, she said, 'The answer is the same to both points. I'm looking for a complete change in my working life. My job in Bristol has become mainly a matter of routine, something I can handle with my eyes closed.' Again she smiled, her eyes holding just a touch of mischief. 'I don't imagine I could ever get to that stage working with you. From what you've told me, I'd have more than enough to keep me busy. I'd welcome that,' she told him sincerely. 'There's very little in my life other than my work and I'm very much in need of a challenge.'

Alec didn't show it but he was taken aback by her last sentence. She had very little in her life other than her work? This girl? 'Mrs Simson—er—may I ask how long you've been widowed?'

'Over three years. I started work with Silver & Silver six months after my husband died.' She lowered her eyes. Her husband. Oh, how very briefly David had been her husband! It was *that* which hurt more than anything, even more than his absence, that which she regretted bitterly—the pitifully short time they had had together as man and wife.

'I see.' Alec nodded. He was beginning to understand. Cherry Simson had made up her mind to become a career girl after her husband's death. Well, that's just the type he wanted, needed. Someone dedicated. And he had now seen the enthusiasm she'd lacked earlier. Or maybe she hadn't, actually. Maybe he'd been wrong. She was a cool customer, this one, not the type to show on her face all that was going on inside her, which was something else in her favour because there were frequent crazy days here at H.O., madly busy days when a level-headed secretary was an invaluable asset.

The interview didn't last long after that. Mr Moore's next question was concerning the computer on a desk on the far side of his spacious office. No, Cherry had no experience with computers; the regional offices did not yet merit their installation.

'Karen sometimes uses it as a word processor,' he informed her. 'Of course we have a typing pool here, on the second floor, but the typing of reports and estimates and the like are easily dealt with on the computer, using the word processing programme. I use it a great deal—as a computer,' he added, smiling. 'I've no doubt there'll be occasions when we'll both want to work on the wretched thing at the same time! However, not to worry. We'll send you on a training course—for three days, probably—and you'll have the hang of it in no time.'

He was talking as though he were offering her the job, Cherry noted, and even when he put it into words for her she still couldn't believe her luck.

'I've been interviewing for the past four days, Cherry, and you were the last person I had to see, so I'm able to tell you that the job is yours if you want it.'

'I do!' She quite forgot herself then, she was so pleased. 'I mean, well, thank you, Mr Moore, I accept!'

'Alec.' He got to his feet, offering her his hand. 'Make it Alec, will you?' They were moving towards the door, confirming that they would put the respective offer and acceptance in writing and go through the usual formalities.

'You'll have to start flat-hunting now, I suppose.' On reaching the door to his office, Alec paused, noting the grace with which she moved. In her deportment, her dress, her voice, this girl was every inch the part.

'As a matter of fact, no. This really is my lucky day!' She smiled up at him. At five feet seven, wearing two inch heels, she could not be described as short. But Alec Moore was around six feet tall, she supposed. He dressed well, too. He was one of those people one would describe as a snappy dresser. The cut of his suit was superb, though his tie was a little loud against the background of a blue shirt. 'A friend of my father's—my father is a dentist——' she threw in irrelevantly, 'is going to work abroad for a year. He's married and he and his wife have a small but very attractive terraced house in Hampstead. Anyhow, they intend to let the place, fully furnished, while they're away, but they're very dubious about what sort of tenants they might get. Even with references, one can't be too careful——'

'And because you're the daughter of a friend, they'd be only too pleased if you took the place on.'

The violet eyes were positively alight with enthusiasm now. 'At a very reasonable rent. Well, affordable at any rate!' Fully furnished houses of this calibre did not come cheaply in London but with her new job there was also a considerable increase in salary.

She said goodbye to Karen Black on the way out, wishing her all the best for the future, and headed for the lift with a light-heartedness she hadn't felt for a very long time. In fact she was a little dazed as she stepped out of the building and into the warm, September sunshine, her mind busily going over the immediate future and the changes it would bring to her life.

Glancing at her watch, she hurried down the steps leading from the front entrance, eager to meet up with her parents and tell them the news which would please them even more than it pleased her. Her progress was halted abruptly and painfully, however, when she walked smack bang into what felt like a brick wall. She staggered backwards, only just managing to stay on her feet, vaguely aware that it was a human being who'd run into her.

Winded, bewildered, she bent to retrieve the small bag which had been knocked from her hands and found herself looking at a pair of masculine feet in expensive leather shoes.

'Why the devil don't you watch where you're going!' A deep, harsh voice barked the question at her. But its owner gave her no time to answer, or rather, to retaliate. What a nerve! *He* had run into *her*! And it hurt!

As she straightened, anger at his rudeness flashing in

her eyes, he stepped away from her without so much as a word of apology, giving her time to register nothing more than his extraordinary height. She felt as though she'd collided with a man-mountain. 'I was about to ask you the same question!' She had intended to shout after him but the words emerged as little more than a hiss. Still, he might have caught them. She hoped so. She turned away from the retreating figure as it stalked through the glass doors of the building and she pondered about him only long enough to wonder whether he was a customer. She hoped not, even though the mishap was entirely his fault.

Cherry thought lady luck had excelled herself when she spotted what she fleetingly mistook for a taxi at the curbside. But that would have been asking too much! She laughed at herself as she realised that the big black vehicle was not a taxi but a Rolls Royce, with a chauffeur sitting patiently behind the wheel!

Shrugging, she hurried in the direction of the restaurant where her parents would be waiting for her, her hand reaching to rub her shoulder, which was suddenly feeling the full benefit of the solid mass which had walked into her.

# CHAPTER TWO

CHERRY picked up the telephone before getting into bed. She must ask reception to give her an alarm call in the morning. The last thing she wanted was to be late on her first day at her new job, and her alarm clock was among her belongings at the house she was renting. It was stupid of her not to have remembered to bring it to the hotel.

Having to spend her first week in a hotel in London was the only hitch in arrangements which had otherwise gone beautifully. The house she was renting had only one bedroom and her father's friend and his wife were not due to leave the country until Friday, so Cherry had had the choice of sleeping on their settee or staying in a hotel. She had opted for the latter, thinking it a bad idea to risk uncomfortable sleep when she would need all her energy for work.

Ten minutes later, having turned off the lamp, she got out of bed and was heading for the bathroom. She'd forgotten to clean her teeth and she giggled about it, wondering what her dentist father would have to say about that! It was a definite indication of how preoccupied she was with thoughts of tomorrow.

'Let's face it, Cherry, you're nervous!' It was a strange thing to be glad about, feeling nervous, but it pleased her; it meant that she was alive and as normal as anyone else.

Satisfied at the thought, she got back into bed and switched off the lamp for the second and last time. Within minutes she was asleep.

When reception rang to wake her up, Cherry was already dressed and made-up. She thanked them and took a long look in the full-length mirror on the wardrobe door. In a black pencil skirt and a crisp white blouse, frilled at the high neckline and at the cuffs, she looked just right. Her hair was swept up into the soft style she usually wore for work and, apart from her deep red lip gloss, her make-up was not obvious. It never was, even when she was going out for the evening—though she could count on one hand the number of times she'd gone anywhere special since David died.

It would happen here, just as it had happened at the regional office. She would be asked out. Dates would be offered ... and politely refused. She simply wasn't interested. Even if there came into her life a man who could measure up to David, come *close* to measuring up to David, she still wouldn't be interested. When he died, he had taken her heart with him.

She looked at her face in the mirror, deliberately clearing the frown which had creased her brow. Moistening her lips, she put a smile on her face, appreciating the difference it made to her appearance. Many a time she had been told what a lovely smile she had, what gorgeous teeth she had, and many a time she had been told that she didn't smile often enough. Well, she would bear that in mind from now on.

The sun was shining. It was early October but the sun was shining from a clear blue sky and she decided she would walk to work instead of taking the Underground. It absolutely wasn't worth taking her car into the centre of London. Picking up the jacket which matched the skirt she was wearing, she went in search of breakfast.

It was still only ten minutes past eight when she walked through the doors of Head Office. So much for her delaying tactics in walking to work. She wasn't due to start till nine. Neither was the receptionist, by the look of things. There was no one behind the reception desk in the foyer. Still, she had been warned by Alec Moore that her hours would by no means be fixed, that there would be times when she would have to stay late, start early.

The lift doors parted on the fifth floor and Cherry walked to her office, remembering clearly which door it was. She opened her office door to be met by silence. Nor was there any noise coming from the room on the other side of the adjoining door. Alec wasn't here yet.

Ten minutes later she had been through the contents of her desk drawers, flicked the switches on the switchboard to direct all calls to her phone, filled the coffee percolator and was checking that her desk diary tallied with that of her boss. She looked through both diaries to the end of the year, noting that Alec had a holiday booked for the first two weeks of December.

Good for Karen; she had left everything as up-to-date and as neat as she could. She had also left with one of the paintings from the wall, a colourful print Cherry had admired when waiting to be interviewed. Despite the freshly decorated appearance of the office, the missing painting had left a mark which was nothing short of unsightly, but that was no problem. She had just the thing to take its place, an original oil painting which had been a wedding present to her and David. She had already taken it to what would soon be her new home and she would call for it tonight. She might just as well enjoy it in her office as in her bedroom.

She was putting her boss's diary back on his desk when she heard a door close in her own office. She jumped, glancing at her watch to see that it was eight-thirty. Was it her boss?

There was nobody there. She stood, frowning, frowning until she realised that it had been the other communicating door which had slammed shut, and not the outer door. She investigated at once, opening the door to find herself in another vacant office considerably bigger than her own. There were two desks in here, each with an electronic typewriter on them, and there were several chairs and a photocopying machine. Her eyes went to the door facing the one she had come through and she investigated further.

That was a mistake. The next office was occupied by someone who had clearly been working for some time, judging by the empty coffee cup on his desk and the papers around it.

'Good morning, Anne.'

'Oh! I'm so sorry. I thought——'

They had both spoken at once. It all happened so quickly—too quickly for Cherry to register immediately who it was she had walked in on. Only then did the man look up, realising his mistake, and Cherry's eyes widened as everything fell shockingly into place.

Clear green eyes regarded her with obvious distaste. 'You!'

The man stood as he snapped out the single word and Cherry took an involuntary step backward. Oh, no! *No!* What an unfortunate way for her new career to begin! Almost a month had passed since the day of her interview but the man she had collided with outside the building had obviously not forgotten what she looked like. And he wasn't a customer of the company, he was Leon Silver, *the Chairman and Managing Director!*

The geography of the offices clicked into place in her mind like a jigsaw puzzle. When one stepped out of the lift, wasn't the first door on the left marked with this title, this name? *His* name!

She looked up at him as he took two steps in her direction, and this time it really was a question of looking up. Leon Silver was way over six feet tall, dwarfing her despite her high-heeled court shoes. Cherry's nervousness increased drastically, taking hold of her with a vengeance. It was not the fact that he was the head of the company, nor was she distressed at the memory of their collision—after all, that was his fault, not hers. It was his countenance that disturbed her so. What a formidable man! He was too tall, too big, too— altogether too *vital.*

Leon Silver leaned lazily against a filing cabinet. His white shirt was open at the neck, his tie dragged to one side. He folded his arms across the massive expanse of a chest which was encased in a close-fitting waistcoat which matched his dark trousers. His body was taut and solid—big, certainly, but there was no excess weight on him.

His eyes flicked over Cherry in a head-to-foot survey which took only a split second. 'Well?' he demanded. 'It seems you're not content with barging into my person, you've taken it upon yourself to barge into my office, too. You might at least state your business—after telling me who you are.'

A horrible feeling swept rapidly over her like a sudden, tropical rainfall. Suddenly she knew, she just *knew* that things were not going to work out as she hoped. There was already a blot on the horizon. Or rather, on her copybook.

This thought was followed, however, by the instantaneous realisation that she could change that, provided she acted quickly and wisely. It came to her instinctively rather than by a process of logic, which she had no time to indulge in. 'I'm so sorry I walked in on you, Mr Silver,' she said, making a subtle but important alteration to the words he'd used. 'I'd heard someone in my office, you see, and I came to investigate.' Even before she finished, she was offering him her hand in a gesture which appeared to be confident, which almost challenged him to refuse it. 'It is Mr Silver, isn't it?'

It worked. He shook her hand for the brief amount of time it took for her to speak her name, which was more than enough for her to be even further disconcerted by him. This man's handshake was more like the grip of a vice and his confirmation of his identity was a bad-tempered grunt. As he let go of her hand, his eyes flickered to her left hand and paused fleetingly on the rings on her wedding finger.

'I'm Alec Moore's new secretary,' she went on, pleased to find that it was within her power to smile at him.

A black eyebrow rose cynically. 'So I gathered. Welcome to the team, Mrs Simson.'

'Thank you.' Her reply was as hollow as his words had been. He had been rude to her a month ago and he was being rude to her now, despite his so-called welcome. Added to that, he was sizing her up as surely as eggs were eggs. And he was doing it not by looking her over but by looking into her eyes as though he could read what went on in her thoughts.

She had the presence of mind to tell herself that he couldn't. Nevertheless, those startlingly green eyes of his were disturbing to say the least. Cherry broke the contact by retreating to her own office, only partially satisfied with the way she'd conducted herself. She had intended to show the man that she was not overawed, that she was not easily intimidated, and she had the feeling she'd failed to do that. She had been polite, she'd made no reference to their first encounter, tempting though it had been to put him straight, yet she was left in no doubt that the Chairman of the company disapproved of her already. And that was unfortunate since she would be working within his orbit. It was also grossly unfair of him. Still, given time she would cancel out that disapproval by sheer efficiency and ... and *bother* the man! she thought impatiently. He had successfully taken the glow off her first day with his obnoxious attitude.

Sitting down at her desk, she mentally labelled and filed Leon Silver under D for Dislike.

In the next instant she was telling herself off. She ought not to decide she disliked the man, not this quickly, not when she was thinking him unfair for labelling and filing *her* under D for Disapproval. She must keep an open mind about him, categorise him only when she knew him well enough to do so. It was nothing short of childish to be thinking of him in terms of his being unfriendly and forbidding.

Cherry closed her eyes, easily conjuring up a mental

picture of him. It was no use. He *was* forbidding, formidable. He was about the same age as Alec Moore, she guessed, somewhere in his early forties, but unlike Alec he was not good-looking. His skin tone was dark, his hair as black as ebony and showing the first hint of greying, but his features were hawk-like, craggy. His was certainly a face one would remember, though, because it was as striking as the rest of him. She shuddered in distaste. Macho types like that always gave her the shudders, especially when they were so blatantly insensitive.

The door from the corridor opened and Alec Moore came in, bright, breezy and smiling. 'Good morning, Cherry, and welcome!'

She felt better at once. 'Good morning. Have you had a nice week-end?'

'I certainly have! In Paris, as a matter of fact. Lovely city, have you ever been there?'

Cherry's smile didn't falter. 'No,' she said quietly. 'No, I haven't.' But she had almost got to Paris ... once. Part of her honeymoon would have been spent in Paris if ... if things had gone according to plan.

Alec walked through to his own office and Cherry followed him. 'Now, the first thing you must do in the morning is to put the coffee on.'

'It's on,' she grinned. 'It'll be ready any minute.' She'd found the coffee in the bottom drawer of her desk (if it hadn't been there, she'd have looked in the stationery cupboard), and discovered where the ladies' room was in her quest for water.

'Good.' Her new boss dropped his briefcase on his desk and flicked it open. 'If I remember correctly, Norman Buckley is coming to see me at eleven ... I'd better make a start.' He picked up his internal phone and tapped out two numbers. 'Anne? Alec. Good morning to you. What's up? You don't sound ... I see. It happens, Anne, it happens. Look, my new secretary's with me now and I wondered if you'd do me a favour and introduce her around. I've got Norman Buckley coming at eleven and some more work to do on his quotation before he gets here, so I can't spare the time to take Cherry on a guided tour.'

He listened, nodded and put the phone down with a word of thanks. 'That was Leon Silver's secretary, Anne Mellor. She said if you'll give her half an hour or so, she'll come to you and show you around. She's a nice girl,' he added, 'I'm sure you'll get on well with her.'

Cherry hoped so. If she got on as well with Anne as she did with Anne's boss, it really would be a disaster. But Anne wouldn't be around for long, would she? Of course Cherry said nothing but she noticed that Alec didn't mention that the other girl was pregnant and would be leaving the company.

It was almost ten o'clock when Anne made the short journey from her office to Cherry's. 'Mrs Simson? It's Cherry, isn't it? Sorry I couldn't come sooner, Mr Silver's daily list was a little longer than usual,' she said, making little sense to Cherry. What was a daily list? List of what?

'How do you do?' Cherry offered her hand, surprised to see that Anne Mellor was in her middle or late thirties. She was a petite woman, very smartly dressed and showing no sign of being pregnant. Her dark hair was short and neat, and while her appearance was impeccable, she seemed weary in spite of the early hour. But the younger girl had no way of knowing whether she always looked like that or whether she really was tired. She certainly didn't have that glow about her which pregnant women are said to have.

Anne Mellor didn't have the warmth of Karen Black. Her attitude was vaguely aloof, though she did take the trouble to explain who was who and precisely what they did as she and Cherry moved from office to office on the fifth floor. 'The dining rooms are on the first floor and lunch is served between eleven-thirty and two-thirty.' They were rounding the corner to their own offices now. 'The photocopying room is in the basement—leave any jobs you want doing in your out-tray and the messenger will collect them and bring them back to you. Use the machine in my office for your small photocopying jobs, though. It's quicker. Come on, I'll show you my office and introduce you to Mr Silver now.'

'Actually, I've——' Cherry got no further. Leon Silver was in Anne's office, talking to a girl who was sitting at the second desk, her fingers on the home keys of her typewriter as she nodded at the instructions she was getting from him, her eyes looking positively alarmed. Cherry felt immediate sympathy for her. The girl was frightened of him, a blind man could have seen that.

'Ah, Mr Silver, may I introduce Mrs Simson, Cherry Simson? She's——'

'Don't bother,' he drawled, cutting off his secretary in mid-flow. 'Mrs Simson and I have already met.' Shrewd green eyes went directly to Cherry's and held for the merest instant before dismissing what they saw.

'Oh!' Anne turned to look at Cherry, who just smiled and said nothing, by which time the big man had vanished into his own office and closed the door behind him. 'And have you met my assistant,' Anne went on, 'Penny Davies? Penny's been with us for three months now . . .'

There were a number of questions Cherry was itching to ask Anne Mellor which had nothing to do with office procedure. Was Leon Silver always such a bear or did he have a touch of the Monday morning blues? Did he harbour grudges, and if so, would he continue to disapprove of her merely because she had walked in on him without knocking?

Alec's visitor left at eleven-forty, at which point the intercom on Cherry's desk buzzed and she flicked the switch. 'Yes, Alec?'

'There are a few letters I want to get in the post

tonight. Will you bring in your notebook, please? And will you——' As he was speaking, the door from Anne's office opened and Leon Silver walked through with a curt, 'Is Alec alone?' to Cherry. She nodded and carried on typing; there was no point in going to Alec for dictation when the other man was with him.

While the door to Alec's office was momentarily open, Cherry heard the two men greet one another. The door closed shut. Then, to her chagrin, she found herself listening to a conversation she wasn't meant to hear. Due to the interruption, Alec had left his intercom switch down and every word the two men spoke was being relayed.

Leon Silver started it with, 'Where's she from? The dizzy brunette out there.'

'Dizzy?' The surprise in Alec's voice was plain to hear. 'Cherry? I can think of a dozen adjectives to describe that young woman, Leon, but dizzy would not be one of them!'

Cherry smiled, pleased by Alec's defence of her. She was about to put an end to her unintended eavesdropping by turning off her own intercom but the MD's next remark stopped her.

'I thought you wouldn't consider having a married woman as your secretary? How come your policy's suddenly changed—or have I to use my imagination?'

'She's a widow. She was Bob Langley's secretary at the Bristol office. Worked there for three years. Since her husband died.'

'A *widow*?' The surprise was evident in Leon Silver's voice now. 'For heaven's sake, how old is she?'

'Twenty-four.'

There was a momentary silence. Cherry looked suspiciously at the intercom, wondering what non-verbal communication was taking place between the two men.

'She's certainly nice to look at, eh, Leon?' There was a hint of laughter from Alec—but no answer from the other man. 'I hope she proves to be as efficient as she's attractive.'

There was a note of impatience in the MD's voice now. 'Look, have you remembered that I'll be away next week? I want you to chair the meeting on Tuesday morning.'

'I've remembered. Next week is half-term, isn't it? Where are you taking your family—or are you spending the week at home?'

'The children want to go to Spain. I know, I know. I can't think why, either. Just some idea they've got into their heads.'

'Will you go along with it?' Alec asked.

'I don't see why not. Where we go is as broad as long to me.'

At that point, Cherry flicked the switch. She had heard enough. Her irritation at the first part of the conversation had been replaced by surprise. So Leon Silver was a family man who was willing to indulge his children's fancy by taking them on a holiday to Spain during their half-term break. She was glad to hear it. Maybe he wasn't as hateful as he appeared to be.

In spite of its inauspicious start, Cherry's first week at work was a resounding success. This was mainly due to Alec, though. He praised her frequently, thanked her always when she had completed a task and he never failed to say please when he asked something of her. The effect of this was to give her confidence. Already she felt safe, all doubts and feelings of insecurity having been dispelled by his attitude. He volunteered explanations to her, when he had time to do so, and she felt free to ask as many questions as she needed to ask.

It was just as well Alec was like that because by the end of the week Cherry had learnt that he had an unusual method of working. His desk was invariably smothered in papers—in no particular order—and on the day that she tidied it for him, she set him back a good half hour because he couldn't find anything. She did not tidy up again!

She also learned that it was quite normal for him to work on three things at once, not at the same time, rather he would switch from one task to the next after being interrupted by a call or a visitor. Still, his method worked, and she would get used to it in time.

On a personal level she learned things about him, too. He was a bachelor and he intended to stay that way. This information came from the horse's mouth—the other things, Cherry gleaned from observation. He fancied himself a bit, he was a little vain, and twice during her first week she had been asked to send flowers to two different women.

On the Friday, Anne Mellor suggested they have lunch together and most of their time was spent talking about their jobs. The older woman had been with Silver & Silver Limited for fourteen years and she had worked with Leon Silver for all of them, having been his secretary before he became Managing Director—when, in fact, he was doing Alec's job as Sales Director. At that point Leon's father had been MD and, when Leon took over from him, the old man stayed on as Chairman; he had since retired completely.

'What's he like to work with?' Cherry asked, remembering Karen Black's words. 'I have the impression he'd be a hard task master.' In the week which had gone by, sped by, she had had brief but frequent contacts with Leon Silver, contacts during which they had spoken to one another with absolute economy, saying only what needed to be said and no more. So far, it had been mainly a question of Cherry passing papers from Alec to him because he liked, she'd learned, to cast his eyes over Alec's projects. Frequent informal meetings took place between fifth floor staff and when one of them was held in Alec's office, she'd had to take notes. It lasted all morning and she might just as well have been invisible as far as Leon Silver was concerned.

Anne's fine, dark eyebrows went up in indignation. 'Mr Silver has no time for sloppiness, if that's what you mean. He's a perfectionist. You'll find that he encourages people to use their own initiative and he's in no way dictatorial, despite his position.'

Cherry had to make a conscious effort to prevent her fork from stopping in mid-air. Well! Had she or had she not been put in her place! Anne Mellor's loyalty to her boss was fierce. What had happened to the sourness Karen Black had spoken of? It must have been very short-lived. There was nothing wrong with such loyalty, it was admirable. But had Anne been *honest*?

'You couldn't ask for a better boss,' she went on, making Cherry even more dubious. 'He knows exactly what he wants to achieve and he goes all out to achieve it. I like a man who knows his own mind. And he works extremely hard. He starts at seven, did you know that? And he's here long after everyone else has gone.'

That he worked overtime was not news to Cherry. In an effort to stay on top of things, she herself had started earlier and finished far later than she should have. There had been so much to take in this week and Alec's output of work was huge. There was also the matter of the word processor. Her three-day training, which had been arranged for her in Bristol, was all very well but what she needed now was practice in using the machine, which she knew would be a boon to her when she was fluent on it. Besides, she'd been in no hurry to get back to the hotel in the evenings, though when she did so it was to flop tiredly into bed soon after dinner.

She had been aware of Leon Silver's presence out of normal hours because on two occasions she'd passed him in the corridor at around seven in the evening.

One thing became clear during that lunch time: if Anne had any criticisms of her boss, she was keeping them strictly to herself. She wasn't as reticent when it came to speaking of Alec, however. 'I don't envy you working for Alec Moore. He doesn't seem to have much of a system, does he? How are you finding it?'

'Oh, he has a system,' Cherry said, her own loyalty to the fore. She had not forgotten how Alec had defended her to Leon Silver. 'A system which works for him. And that's all that matters, isn't it, that the work gets done?'

'Mr Silver likes him.' That was all Anne said, the implication being that if Mr Silver liked Alec, she would tolerate him; she was just glad she wasn't working for him.

The same applies, Cherry thought. She was very glad she wasn't working for Anne's boss! It still bothered her though, this feeling that Leon Silver disapproved of her. He was the MD, after all. She put a question to Anne as nonchalantly as she could. 'Has he—has Mr Silver said anything to you about me?'

The older woman frowned. 'Like what?'

'Well—anything at all.' When this was met with a blank look, Cherry gave up. 'I—it's just that I have the feeling he disapproves of me, doesn't like me for some reason.'

There was laughter now. Anne leaned closer, tapping Cherry's hand, but her words came out quite scornfully. 'My dear, if Mr Silver disapproved of you, you'd be out so fast it would make your head spin. Take my word for it, you'd know about it by now.'

'Out? But it was Alec who took me on and he is a company director——'

'Cherry, Leon Silver controls this company. Leon Silver *is* this company. Don't think for one minute that——'

'What is it?' Cherry saw her sway as she sat, her face paling visibly. 'Anne, are you all right?'

'Yes, I——' She straightened. 'I'm okay, just tired. God, I'm tired!'

'Can I do anything?' Cherry asked, anxious for her. 'Would you like a glass of water or——'

'No, no. I'll be okay in a moment. Look, I'm sorry if

I snapped at you. And I haven't helped you much this
week, I simply haven't had time. I wanted to have lunch
with you on Monday but——'

'It's all right. Don't worry about it, any of it.'

Cherry was subjected to a long look which was
followed by an almost imperceptible nod. Anne's face
softened and it was only then that she told Cherry she
was pregnant. The younger woman had the distinct
feeling that she had been subjected to some sort of test
during this lunch hour—a test she had passed. 'Is it
your first?' she asked, already knowing the answer.

'Yes, after years of hoping.' Anne's face was
wreathed in smiles now. They faded after a moment,
and she sighed heavily. 'I'd hoped to work right up to
the end but—I'm not sure I'll be able to. I—think I'll go
home, actually. I'm feeling quite . . . the boss won't
need me this afternoon,' she went on, looking at her
watch and speaking almost to herself now. 'He's
upstairs having lunch with Mrs Reynolds just now . . .'

Cherry didn't know a Mrs Reynolds. 'You mean in
his office? Or is there another dining room upstairs?'

'Mm? No, no. In his apartment.'

'You've lost me, Anne.'

'Sorry. I mean the penthouse, his apartment on the
top floor.'

'Oh! I had no idea——' She'd had no idea there was
a floor beyond the fifth, let alone that the MD lived in a
penthouse apartment. It must be set well back from the
edge of the building, she thought.

Anne was still somewhat distracted, still looking at
her watch as if she were having difficulty reading it. 'He
finishes early on Fridays to collect his children from
boarding school, so I think I can safely go——'

'But are you fit to travel?'

'Yes. I'll take a taxi. Honestly, I'll be all right. All I
need is a rest. Thank goodness I've got next week off!
Mr Silver's going on holiday for a week. Look, Cherry,
he'll be back at his desk by half-past two. He's

expecting a call from Rome then. Will you pop in and see him, explain what's happened?'

'I—of course.' She could hardly refuse. 'Come on, at least let me get your coat and see you into a taxi.'

Alec was looking through her in-tray when Cherry got back to her office. She explained what had happened with Anne and he made sympathetic noises. 'She's having a bad time with morning sickness, poor dear. It'll pass.'

'This was hardly morning sickness!' Cherry couldn't help grinning.

Alec caught her eye and started laughing. 'You're right. But I'm not an authority on these matters.'

'I should hope not! Will you excuse me a moment?' she went on, bracing herself. 'I'd better explain to Mr Silver . . .'

The Chairman's office was not only luxurious it was also neat, always neat. Situated on the corner of the building, it had two large windows under one of which was a leather Chesterfield settee in black. There were four matching chairs, a large glass-topped coffee table and the carpet was the same dark green which covered the corridors. Side by side on one wall there were two old-fashioned portraits of the brothers Silver, Edward and Benjamin, the men who had founded the, then, engineering company nearly one hundred years ago.

At the moment there wasn't a single file, a single piece of paper, on Leon's desk. He was standing by the window when Cherry went in, his hands thrust deeply into his pockets as he looked down at the street below. 'Yes, Mrs Simson?'

She blinked in surprise. Gone was the formal business suit, complete with waistcoat, which he normally wore. Instead he was wearing a maroon roll-neck sweater and black slacks and he looked . . . he looked like a different man, equally imposing—but so different! The sprinkling of grey in his hair looked silver in the light from the window, making a dramatic contrast with the predominant blackness of it.

'I've just put Anne into a taxi.' Cherry felt the full benefit of those penetrating green eyes, even though she was standing several yards away from him. He said not a word about his secretary after she'd told him what had happened, showing neither sympathy nor surprise. He merely nodded.

Cherry turned to go. Why did she always feel that she wanted to get out of his presence as quickly as possible?

'Just a minute, Mrs Simson.'

His tone stopped her in her tracks, gave her the distinct impression that she was not supposed to leave his office until he dismissed her. Bristling, she turned to face him.

He crossed the room slowly and stood about two feet away from her, towering over her. She looked up at him, her violet eyes impassive and meeting his directly. 'Yes?' she asked coolly.

'You've been here a week now. I'd like to know how it's going.'

If his eyes hadn't travelled downwards in such an insolent manner, she'd have answered him reasonably. As it was, he looked her over slowly this time, slowly yet without the slightest spark of interest. Not that she'd have welcomed any interest, it was just—just that he managed somehow to make her feel insulted. It didn't make sense, what he was doing and how she was feeling. Nor did their unspoken antagonism. But it was there. Oh, it was *there*!

She felt suddenly as though she were in danger, which was something else that didn't make sense. 'I—perhaps you should ask Alec that question. He's more likely to give you——'

'I've asked Alec,' he informed her. 'I was interested in your point of view.'

She faltered, feeling ensnared by the gaze from clear green eyes framed by long black lashes. Heavens, *why* was she so stupidly tongue-tied?

'No comment, Mrs Simson? Am I to take it then that you won't be with us for long?'

'Yes. I mean, no. I—I've enjoyed this week very much.'

'You think you'll be able to take the pace?' he asked, in a tone which spoke of his doubts.

It was almost as if he were goading her. But why should he want to do that? She let out an impatient breath, as irritated with herself as she was with him. 'Mr Silver, it will probably take six months for me to see every aspect of what my job entails. May I suggest that you ask me again then?'

A slight smile pulled at the corners of his mouth and he inclined his head, looking at her with unconcealed interest now, and something approaching amusement. 'I'll do that, Mrs Simson ... if you're still around.' His external telephone shrilled and he turned to pick it up with a curt, 'Excuse me.'

Cherry hesitated for a second, not at all sure that this was her cue to leave. She was making her way to the door which led to the corridor when his voice halted her again. 'Mrs Simson. . . .' He put his hand over the receiver, giving her the benefit of his smile for the first time ever, and her eyes went of their own accord to his mouth. She had thought his eyes his most attractive feature, disturbing though they were, but she wasn't sure now. His teeth were white, even, and his smile softened the hawk-like features considerably. It was a strong face, one that had managed to etch itself into her memory as if she had known it for years.

'Have a nice week-end,' he drawled.

Confused, she could do no more than nod. She made her exit with as much speed as gracefulness would allow, aware of the low laughter coming from him as she closed the door. Had he started his telephone conversation or was he laughing at her? Why did she feel as though she'd just been part of a game of cat and mouse—and lost?

By the time she reached the ladies' room, she was fuming. He really was a most unpleasant man! His sarcasm was not exactly overt, yet it couldn't be missed. How on earth had Anne stuck with him for fourteen years? And, come to think about it, would she manage to settle in her new job when she and the Managing Director were experiencing such an awful personality clash?

# CHAPTER THREE

It bothered her all week-end. It was a strange week-end. On the Friday evening, she moved into her new home and busied herself by making little alterations to it. The owners of the house had already hung some of her clothes in the wardrobes for her and had put into the loft several bits and pieces which Cherry didn't particularly want around.

She had brought from Bristol several ornaments, a couple of lamps and three paintings, one of which now hung in her office. She put a stack of records on the hi-fi and moved from room to room, appreciating her good fortune in having a comfortable and colourful house to herself. The kitchen was small but compact, complete with fridge-freezer, washing machine and tumble dryer. The living room was not as Cherry would have furnished and decorated it, but it was nice nonetheless. The curtains were made from midnight blue velvet, and they toned well with the dralon three-piece suite in pale blue. The carpet was fussier, being patterned and a mixture of subdued colours, but it added an air of warmth and cosiness.

At nine o'clock she settled in an armchair and sat quietly, looking at the flames of the gas fire which for all the world resembled a real log fire. Yes, she would be very comfortable here and even if her new job didn't work out well, she would have no trouble finding work elsewhere. She would stay in London; she was no stranger to the capital and she'd always liked the place.

Her parents had phoned her the previous evening to ask whether she was going home for the week-end. She'd told them no, what she really wanted to do was have a rest on Saturday and Sunday. On Saturday morning, however, when there was nothing for her to do by the time eleven o'clock rolled around, she began to think she might drive home after all. She picked up the telephone receiver. Thoughts of Leon Silver were still annoying her and she would very much like to talk about him with someone who could be objective. She put the phone down again. Her parents would hardly be objective, would they? Besides, she was supposed to be showing them that she could cope with anything these days—and this really was a very small crisis! She considered ringing her brother, who lived in Wales, but she abandoned that idea, too.

A brisk walk over Hampstead Heath helped her to put a different slant on things. She was too sensitive, that's all. Half of Mr Silver's sarcasm was probably in her imagination. Maybe he was like that with everyone. Why should she think he'd singled her out? In any case, she got on extremely well with Alec, and that's what was really important.

Over a solitary dinner that evening Cherry realised that her darling David hadn't entered her thoughts once that day. It was an alarming realisation and she didn't interpret it as being a good thing. In her mind and in her heart he was very much alive and she felt almost guilty because she hadn't spared him a thought. She closed her eyes, bringing his face into her mind, hearing his voice laughingly telling her that she worried too much, that she was too sensitive. It was David who'd told her that, time and time again. But he had been sensitive too, a kind, gentle man with whom she had fallen in love the moment she'd set eyes on him. Such things did happen; it had happened to her.

She no longer cried these days. During the years since his death she had wept until there were no tears left. She had gone through a period of anger—at the world, at herself, at the cruel Fate which had taken him from her, even at David himself. She had gone through the 'If only . . .' stage, too, uselessly telling herself that if she and David had made different plans for their honeymoon he would still be alive and she would have had the life which had been so carefully planned with him.

All that remained now was regret. There were too few memories and an excruciating regret that she had never actually shared a life with him as his wife.

Too late. It was too late. God knew that she had counted her regrets often enough and one day, one day, she would perhaps be able to convince herself it was a waste of time and energy, that regrets wouldn't change anything.

The next week at the office was hectic. Leon Silver's absence threw more work in Alec's direction, which in turn added to Cherry's workload. Penny Davies, Anne's young assistant, coped with her boss's phone calls where possible but she had been left with enough work to keep her busy for the week.

Cherry went to Wales at the week-end and met up with her parents at her brother's house. Their grandchild was celebrating his fourth birthday on the Saturday—which was a day of wobbly jellies and sticky cakes and laughter and chaos—and Cherry enjoyed every minute of it!

Trouble struck in the middle of the following week.

She shouldn't have been surprised when she learned that Anne wasn't coming in to work on the Wednesday because she had looked peaky at the start of the week. Still, she didn't care for the way the news was given to her.

She walked into her office at one minute past eight and no sooner had she hung up her coat than the internal telephone buzzed. She picked up the receiver, knowing that at this hour it could only be one person.

'Mrs Simson, I'd like a word with you.'

'Yes, Mr Silver.' There was never a 'please' or 'thank you' from him. Not for her, anyhow.

Vaguely alarmed, she peered unseeingly at the rain

slashing sideways across the windows, delaying long enough to run a comb through her hair. She was wearing it down today, a shiny dark cascade down the centre of her back, clipped at the nape with an ornamental slide. She pulled a mirror from her handbag and took a quick look at her face. It was passable.

The late October winds were biting and she'd travelled to work wearing a full-length coat, but she never wore anything more than a lightweight dress or a skirt and blouse around the office because the air-conditioning system kept the building at a comfortable temperature—a system installed by Silver & Silver, of course! This morning she was wearing a plain black skirt which flattered her slender, gently curved figure, and with it she wore a vivid red silk blouse.

Leon Silver's eyes flicked rapidly over her as he invited her to sit down—checking on the suitability of her appearance, no doubt! She had no idea which part of Spain he'd been to the previous week but he'd come back with a deep suntan which, according to Penny Davies, made him 'Even more attractive.' Cherry had pointed out that that was strictly a matter of opinion.

'I've just had a call from Anne. She isn't coming in today. I think——' He broke off suddenly, content to finish the sentence to himself. He was quiet for so long that Cherry had to prompt him, feeling uncomfortable under the hold of a pair of eyes which were looking at her but no longer really seeing her.

'You were saying, Mr Silver?'

He snapped out of it at once, his deep voice cold and curt as he spoke. 'Yes. You'll be working for me today. It'll make no difference to Alec, since he's in Birmingham for the day.'

Her heart sinking, Cherry said goodbye to the idea of catching up with her own work while Alec was out of town. The flow of work seemed to be getting thicker with every passing day and she had quite a backlog. 'I—er—this is a little awkward, Mr Silver. I've got a backlog of letters on tape which absolutely must be in the post today.' She did *not* add that they should have been in the post yesterday! Thank heavens she'd typed some of them after hours last night!

'Are they confidential?'

'No.'

He looked heavenward, speaking with an exaggerated patience which brought a blush to her normally pale complexion. 'Then send them down to the typing pool. This is called *delegation*, Mrs Simson. Now, you do write shorthand, I suppose? Unlike Alec, I never use dictaphone machines.'

Alec used both, her shorthand skills and his dictaphone. 'Yes, I do but——'

'But?'

But I don't want to work for you, she groaned inwardly. If only this man didn't make her feel so wretchedly self-conscious, she'd have been pleased to help out in Anne's absence. But he did, and she hated the thought of being in such close contact with him for a whole day.

There was boredom in his voice now. 'Mrs Simson, we're wasting time. Either finish your sentence or fetch your notebook.'

She settled for the latter, wishing she could bring herself to say what was on her mind. He made her nervous. She didn't like him one iota. She thought him rude and aggressive. But how could she say all this? She didn't want to lose her job, for heaven's sake! And it would only be for one day, after all ...

Leon Silver started by giving her a long list of telephone calls he wanted her to make for him. He then moved on to internal memos to various department heads and dictated without notes at a steady pace which kept Cherry's pencil flying across the paper. She was a nervous wreck, taking dictation from him, and was infinitely relieved when the telephone rang and she could take a brief respite. Being tactful, she was about to leave the office as he picked up the receiver, but he waved her back into her chair. No sooner had she sat than the other line started to ring and he was waving her towards the outer office to answer it.

She sat down at Anne's desk and picked up the phone. 'Mr Silver's office.'

'Who is that? Is it Anne?' A gravelly, masculine voice asked the question.

'No, this is Cherry Simson. May I help you?'

'Put me though to Leon, please.'

'I'm sorry, Mr Silver's on the other line at the moment——' No, he wasn't! She saw from the switchboard that he'd just hung up. 'Oh, he's just finished speaking, actually. Who's calling?'

'Leon Silver.'

'Yes,' Cherry said politely, thinking the man had misunderstood her. 'And who is it calling?'

There was a smile in his voice. 'This is Leon Silver *senior*.'

'Oh! Ah. Yes, Mr Silver, I'll put you through . . .'

She did so at once—or so she thought. But somehow, somehow, she managed to cut the call off. Groaning inwardly, she waited for a verbal blast from the adjoining office.

There wasn't one.

Leon Silver came in person, stood by the door and just looked at her. 'You said my father was on the line?'

'I—yes. I'm so sorry, I—cut him off. If you'll tell me his number, I'll——'

'Don't bother. I'll do it.'

Cherry let him get on with it. She stayed right where she was, very near to tears. What on earth was wrong with her? Why did she allow herself to be fazed by him like this? He might be the Chairman and Managing Director but he was just a man, just a man like any other man. And she was a mature, level-headed, experienced secretary—so what the devil was wrong with her?

'Mr Silver's office.'

'Who's that? It isn't Anne.' This time, the caller was more positive about her not being Anne, and this time it was a female caller. A husky voice with a hint of a foreign accent asked for Mr Silver.

Cherry went into a similar routine. 'I'm sorry, he's on the other line at the moment, may I take a message?'

'Ask him to ring me back, would you? It's Mrs Reynolds, Heidi Reynolds.'

Cherry frowned. Mrs Reynolds was a name she'd heard once before but she hadn't met anyone by that name. 'Er—which department are you in, Mrs Reynolds?'

'What?' On having the question repeated, she said haughtily, 'I'm not in any "department". I'm a friend of Mr Silver. Ask him to ring me back as soon as possible. He knows where to reach me.' And with that she hung up.

It happened again. No sooner had Cherry put the phone down than another call came in, and it wasn't even nine o'clock yet!

This time her offer of taking a message was accepted and she wrote it all down as it was given to her, word for word. She had just replaced the receiver when Leon did likewise, and she went back into his office and put the message on his desk. 'There were two calls while you were talking to your father. The first one was a Mrs Reynolds who wants you to ring her back as soon as possible, so I'll—er—come back in a few moments, shall I?'

He looked up at her as she hovered, that infuriating, exaggerated patience in his voice as he handed back the written message. 'You may come back when you've transcribed this,' he said. 'Sanskrit is not one of my best subjects, Mrs Simson.'

She blushed furiously. She'd given him the message in shorthand, something she'd never done in all her working life! How stupid of her! But it was *his* fault, his attitude was enough to throw anyone into a quandary.

He picked up the phone as she was retreating from the office, glancing at her and sighing as he started to dial. 'I hope you aren't going to continue like this all day, Mrs Simson. I can't decide whether you're just plain incompetent or whether you've got a severe case of PMT.'

Cherry's mouth fell open but no words came out. For just a second she thought she must be hearing things, even as she knew full well she wasn't. Too angry, too astonished to speak, she marched out of the office and closed the door firmly behind her.

She was fuming, absolutely fuming. But her anger was directed at herself as much as him. She'd been stupid in giving him the benefit of the doubt in the first place. She was too soft and she had an unrealistic faith in human nature, tending to think that all people were nice, really. Well, there was no longer any room for doubt about Leon Silver's sarcasm! None at all!

He wouldn't get the better of her. In that instant, she made up her mind once and for all that Leon Silver would not get the better of her! It had become a matter of pride. Her anger fired her with a determination to prove to that man that his opinion of her and her inability to cope was wrong. Wrong!

It was an awful, nerve-racking, tension-filled day and by the end of it Cherry had aching shoulders and a pain in the neck.

Alec came in at four-thirty. He stayed long enough to sign the letters which she'd retrieved from the typing pool, before dashing off again to keep an appointment with his physiotherapist.

At five past seven she took the balance of Leon Silver's work into his office and put it on his desk. He wasn't around. And for once she didn't stay any later, either.

Feeling absolutely shattered, she covered her typewriter, donned her coat and made her way to the lift. The night watchman was used to her by now and she was predicting with a smile his, 'Working late again, Miss?' But her smile faded as the lift doors opened. It came down from the penthouse and it was occupied by Leon Silver.

Cherry's breath caught in her throat. He was wearing formal evening dress and he looked magnificent, the crisp whiteness of his dress-shirt making a stark contrast against the dark tan of his skin.

'Finished already, Mrs Simson?'

She stepped confusedly into the lift, speaking far more sharply than she intended. 'I do have a home to go to!'

Leon Silver said nothing. He didn't need to. He punched the ground floor button and the doors of the lift drew silently together.

Cherry couldn't take her eyes off him. She was able to look at him, unobserved, via the mirror which covered the lift wall. She didn't actually know how old he was but he looked younger this evening, younger and yet distinguished. The sprinkling of grey in his thick, dark hair was attractive and she noticed the way it curled at the bottom, just behind his ear. She looked away then, only to find that her eyes were drawn back to the mirror.

His overall appearance was dramatic, his presence impossible to ignore. His stance held more than pride in it, it was that of a man who enjoyed his exceptional height, a man who had total confidence in himself in every respect. The set of his head told of even more—it was bordering on arrogance. And yes, she had to concede, reluctantly, that he was attractive. Whether it was in spite of these things or because of them, she couldn't be sure. But Penny had been right, the Chairman and Managing Director of the company was an attractive man. Very. What a pity it was only skin deep!

She couldn't help wondering how his wife got on with him. And where was she now? Where was he going, all dressed up like this, without his wife?

'And where would that be?' he asked suddenly, turning his head towards the mirror so that his eyes met hers, catching her in her scrutiny of him.

Cherry dragged her eyes from the mirror, only to find they went directly to his. She felt warmth creeping up her face and she was furious with herself, ridiculously grateful when the lift came to a halt and the doors opened. It had been too much, standing with him in the confines of the lift. It was her greatest desire to keep her distance from this man both mentally and physically—if the latter could be achieved in the circumstances. 'I beg your pardon?'

He'd already started walking towards the entrance to the building and she was three paces behind him. 'Your home. Where is it?'

'Hampstead.'

'Good evening, Mr Silver.' The night watchman was there, holding the door open for them. 'Good evening, Miss. Working late again, I see.'

Cherry flashed him a smile just as Leon paused to talk to him, effectively blocking her exit. 'Hello, Bill. How's the family?'

'Oh, they're all well, thanks. And yours?'

'Yes. Everyone's fine, thank you. See you later.'

Well! Such civility! The night watchman had looked at Leon Silver as though he were the best thing since sliced bread. He obviously didn't know his boss very well.

No sooner had she finished the thought than she was in for another surprise. Leon turned, having remembered that she was alive, and let her pass before him. She started to button her coat. The wind had dropped but it was still raining, a steady drizzle now.

'Where in Hampstead, exactly?'

A black Rolls Royce drew up at the curb just as she answered him, a car she remembered seeing once before, and his offer of a lift was the last thing she expected—or wanted. And there again, it wasn't an offer so much as an order.

'Get in. I'll drop you off.'

'Thank you, but no thank you,' she said smoothly, lying in her teeth. 'I have some shopping to do.'

He nodded shortly, striding down the steps with a barely audible, 'Goodnight, Mrs Simson.'

It was silly of her to derive such satisfaction from her refusal of a lift, but she did. Her pride had taken over again. She watched as the car pulled smoothly away, knowing the tiniest regret. She'd never been in a Rolls Royce, but sitting next to Leon Silver for the ride was more than she was prepared to pay for the experience.

Shrugging, she turned her collar up against the rain and it was only then that she realised she'd left her brolly in the office.

'Forgotten something, Miss?' The night watchman smiled broadly. 'Not going back to work, are you?'

'No chance, Bill! Not tonight.'

He was there again when she came back, brolly in hand. 'How do you like your new job? Getting on all right, are you? This is a good firm to work for. I've been with them eleven years, used to work in the other building before they moved into this one.'

Cherry stopped to have a chat with him, something he was evidently keen on. She didn't mind, there was nothing and nobody waiting for her at home, and Bill's job must be a lonely one.

'I was saying to Graham O'Connell only the other day——'

'Graham O'Connell?'

'Mr Silver's chauffeur,' he supplied. 'Well, he's chauffeur-cum-butler-cum-handyman, really. Lives upstairs with the boss, has done since his wife died. He's a fine man, isn't he?'

'I don't know, Bill. I haven't met him.'

The elderly watchman looked at her blankly. 'I'm not sure what you mean, Miss.'

'Mr Silver's chauffeur, I've never met him.'

'Oh, no, I meant Mr *Silver*. I was saying what a fine

man he is, very much like his father. Course I know him, too. Now there's a man who . . .'

It seemed that Cherry's tiredness had reached her brain. Who was Bill talking about now, Silver junior or Silver senior? It took several more seconds for her to realise the extent to which they'd been at cross purposes. 'Bill, you just said something about his wife having died . . .'

'Five years ago. An awful business. The children would be—what? About three, I suppose. 'Course, she and the children didn't live in the penthouse, and he only used it on odd nights then. They all lived in Buckinghamshire, where Mr Silver senior lives now. Well, not in the same house, of course . . .

She managed to sort it out, just. So it was *Leon*'s wife who'd died five years ago, not the chauffeur's. She glanced towards the door as though she would see him standing there as he had just a short time ago, a feeling of sympathy for him pulling her eyebrows together. So Leon Silver was a widower . . .

Bill caught the look and misinterpreted it. 'I'm sorry, Miss, I didn't mean to keep you——'

'No, no, that's okay.' She paused, curious. 'He—hasn't remarried . . .' She put it as though it were a statement, not a question. She didn't want the watchman to realise how little she knew, nor did she want to appear to be quizzing him.

'Not as yet. Shame, really. It'd be nice for those nippers to have a mother again. They're lovely kids. Have you seen them yet?'

'No.'

'Twin girls. They'll be eight now, I suppose.'

Eight years old—and they were already in boarding school. It seemed very young to Cherry. 'Mr Silver brings them home at the week-ends, though,' she said, following the thought through.

'Oh, yes, Miss. He picks 'em up every Friday and takes them to the family home—his father's house, I mean. They spend the odd week-end upstairs, but not often. Still, you'll meet them sometime. Sweet kids, they are, identical, you know. I couldn't tell one from the other when I last saw them!'

She joined in his mirth and extracted herself a few minutes later, mulling over what she'd learned. Poor little devils, fancy being sent to boarding school at such a tender age. And how long had they been there?

She walked briskly towards the Underground, her sympathy for Leon Silver having fizzled out completely. He wouldn't want children around. He preferred to spend thirteen hours a day working.

And how he worked! She thought about the company and she thought about the twins. It was obvious which was the more precious to him.

Wasn't that just *typical* of a man like Leon Silver!

# CHAPTER FOUR

'ARE you looking forward to your holiday, Alec?'

'What do you think?' Alec Moore leaned back in his chair and stretched his legs. He had a hundred things to do before he left the office tonight and he knew that his meal with Cherry would last longer than an hour. But he'd just invited her out to lunch because she'd worked damned hard in the two months she'd been with him and he felt it was the least he could do by way of showing his appreciation.

He smiled inwardly. That wasn't strictly true, he also wanted to learn more about her. She interested him. He couldn't weigh her up. He'd felt this way when he'd interviewed her and he still wasn't much the wiser. Oh, he'd learned a lot about her nature, that she wasn't the cool customer he'd thought her. She was quietly spoken, a gentle girl, but that wasn't the same thing. She wasn't really tough enough for the job she was in— she was too sensitive, easily hurt, lacking confidence, but she made a valiant effort to hide all of these things and she thought nobody was aware of them. In other words, she was a lovely girl both outwardly and inwardly, and she was intelligent. What did it matter if he had to make a deliberate effort to give her plenty of encouragement? That was no problem at all.

She was, he thought, a stunner. What a pity she was so much younger than he ... He laughed at himself. He wouldn't stand a cat's chance in hell with a girl like Cherry Simson. From what he could gather, and it wasn't much, she had not the slightest interest in the opposite sex. She was still in love with her husband, poor kid. He realised that much even though she never, ever, mentioned the man's name. More than once he

51

had tried tactfully to quizz her about what had happened to him but she closed up like a clam.

She didn't go out much, either. She was still working till seven or eight in the evening and only twice had she mentioned that she'd been out to see a show—alone. Her week-ends seemed to be spent doing her housework or her washing or something—or visiting her parents or her brother and his family. What a waste, what a bloody waste!

'Have you ever been skiing before?' she asked, her violet eyes dancing with laughter at the way he'd answered her last question. He had his back to the window, was sitting behind his desk, and Cherry was facing him. But the harshness of the morning light was no worry for this girl. It did wonders for her. He could imagine what her face would look like by candlelight . . . but he'd prefer to find out . . .

'How's that for a figure!' He'd made the remark half-jokingly to Leon a couple of weeks ago, the day Cherry had been wearing that little black dress and was bending over her desk as she wrote down a phone message. The door of the office was open and both men could see her.

But Leon had merely flung down the file he'd borrowed and muttered, 'You're turning into a lecher in your old age, Alec. If she's a distraction to you, you shouldn't have hired her in the first place. Take my advice, don't mix business with pleasure—if that's what you have in mind.'

'What's the matter with you?' Alec had retorted, taken aback at the other man's sharpness. 'Don't you appreciate a beautiful girl as much as the rest of us? And what's wrong with a little imagining now and then?'

Actually, no one could accuse Leon of lacking imagination or of not appreciating beauty. He'd probably just got out of bed on the wrong side that day and left his sense of humour under his pillow. His relationship with Heidi Reynolds must surely stimulate both his imagination and his appreciation! Now there was a sexy woman, Heidi Reynolds, twice divorced and with her sights set firmly on Leon as a third husband. And Leon could do worse—a lot worse!

Alec sat up. He would *not* ask Cherry to dine with him that evening. He'd been toying with the idea, thinking he'd see how lunch went first . . . but Leon had given him good advice. Mixing business with pleasure, especially with his own secretary, was an unwise thing to do.

'Cherry,' he grinned, 'you're looking at an expert! After these two weeks in Switzerland I'll probably reach Olympic standard!'

Cherry giggled at him. He was such a nice man! She was so lucky to be working with him. During the last two months she'd become more and more fluent with her work and even the madness of the past few days hadn't thrown her. When the regional sales figures had come in last month, she'd felt she was drowning under a workload she would never get through. But this month, this week, it had been different, she had coped very well. Today was Friday and taking ten minutes off to have coffee with Alec, at his invitation, was not causing her to worry how she might otherwise be spending the time; everything was under control.

And he'd just invited her out to lunch by way of thanking her for her efforts. Oh, how *much* that did for her confidence! She was settled in her job now, and successful . . . at least as far as Alec was concerned.

What the Managing Director thought of her these days, she didn't know. Since the day she'd had to work for him, her life had been busy but peaceful. Anne had taken no more time off, was looking much better these days—and considerably thicker around the waist!—so Cherry's exposure to Leon Silver had reverted to the norm. She saw him daily, of course, but they were back to that safe economy of conversation and her manner towards him was one of cool politeness.

She felt almost light-hearted as she touched up her make-up in the ladies' room just before twelve, looking forward to lunch with her boss, looking forward to a week-end with her parents. They were coming to her this time and she'd booked tickets for a new West End play on the Saturday evening.

In the morning, she was going on a shopping spree with her mother. Her salary cheque was as yet untouched and she planned on spending most of it on clothes. She hadn't bought a thing since she'd been in London and it was high time she took advantage of the West End shops. There'd certainly been no time for that during her lunch times! They lasted half an hour at the most. Not that she minded.

'Ready, Cherry?'

'Ready!'

Alec helped her into her coat and they made their way to the lift, chatting about his flight to Switzerland the following morning. The doors were just about to close on them when a deep voice called, 'Hold it!', the call button was punched, the doors opened again and Leon Silver joined them.

Nods and looks were exchanged and for several seconds nobody spoke. Leon Silver changed that, his eyes almost glacial as he addressed Cherry. 'Well,' he drawled, 'I'm sure this will be a nice send off for Alec.'

'I'm sorry?' She shivered inwardly at the coldness of his clear green eyes, at the cynical smile touching his mouth.

'Having lunch with you, Mrs Simson. I mean it'll make a nice start to his holiday. Won't it, Alec?' He looked at the other man, his smile broadening but not reaching his eyes. 'You are taking your secretary to lunch, aren't you?'

'I am.'

'A business lunch, is it?'

'No, it isn't.' Alec was irritated and not afraid to show it. 'It's by way of thanking Cherry for her hard work these past two months.'

'I'm sure it is.'

'She's doing a good job,' Alec went on, adding pointedly, 'and a little appreciation never goes amiss, Leon.'

'So they tell me. But there again, if it's over done, it could be misconstrued. Wouldn't you agree, Alec?'

Cherry was looking from one man to the other, acutely aware of an undercurrent but at a loss to understand it. It could only be that Leon Silver disagreed with Alec when he said she was doing a good job. What a hateful man you are, she thought, her own eyes growing colder as she looked at the back of his head. And what do you know, anyhow? I only worked for you for one day and you didn't give me a chance to breathe, let alone get everything right! You hateful, mountainous cynic!

Dear Lord, it was just as though he picked up her thoughts then, the way he turned suddenly to look at her! 'I'm sorry, Mrs Simson, did you just say something?'

'Not a word.' She spoke coolly but her nerves were jangling like mad and she felt as though she'd just told a lie. This man's shrewdness was unnerving. This man was unnerving, full-stop.

He got out at the second floor, thankfully, leaving Cherry and Alec to pick up the thread of the conversation they'd been having. Neither of them mentioned his attitude or even his name; integrity would not allow that.

'Darling, you told us all that half an hour ago!' The protest came from Cherry's father just as they were finishing dinner that evening.

Had she really been moaning about Leon Silver for half an hour? 'I'm sorry, Daddy, but I can't help it. He is so *irritating*!' She plonked her coffee cup back on its saucer and tried hard to be more rational. 'All right, perhaps I should say he irritates *me*. Nobody else complains about him, granted, but as far as I'm concerned—well, he seems to have it in for me.'

'Have it in for you?' her mother echoed. 'But why should he? What do you mean?'

Cherry had told them of Leon Silver's sarcasm and of the conversation in the lift that day, but they still didn't seem to understand properly. Her father said she was reading things into the MD's words and her mother suggested he'd probably been annoyed with his Sales Director for picking that particular day to take her out to lunch. Nonsense! What difference did the day of the week make? Alec had been right up-to-date with his work by the time he'd left the office in the evening. She'd been there, she knew, she'd stayed with him till six.

She had then dashed home and made dinner for her parents. And she was probably boring them now, going on about Leon Silver. She changed the subject. Well, slightly. She continued to talk about work because they were interested in her job, but she didn't mention the Managing Director's name again. Nor would she for the rest of the week-end.

'Christmas,' she said a little later. 'Have you decided what's happening? Are Kevin and Julie doing it or are you?' Strictly speaking it was her brother's turn to cater for Christmas, but his wife, Julie, was six months pregnant and that had no doubt been taken into account.

'We are.' It was a chorus.

'I thought so.' Cherry smiled. 'So we're all congregating at your house. Well, I'm pleased to say I'll be having the usual week off.'

'Will you be bringing anyone with you?' her mother wanted to know. She shook her head.

'What about New Year's Eve?' Her father glanced at her mother and back to her, smiling. 'You've probably got something planned here in London, have you?'

It was a deliberately pointed question and both Michael Marshall and his wife knew the answer full well. 'No, Daddy, I haven't.' Cherry looked down at the white lace tablecloth. Her parents were too obvious at times. They might just as well ask her outright whether she was dating someone, whether she'd met in London the man who might take over where her husband left off.

They did ask her outright. 'Haven't you been out with anyone at all? Now don't try telling us you haven't been asked!'

Patiently, her love for them overcoming her irritation, she said, 'No, I won't tell you that. I've been asked out by several men at work and by my next door neighbour here.' Her eyes twinkled. 'My neighbour's a male model, would you believe? He's too perfectly beautiful to be interesting and much too full of himself for my liking!'

Her smiles were not reciprocated. There was a short, awkward silence.

'Give me time,' she said quietly. 'Give me time and we'll just see . . . well, I'm just taking each day as it comes.'

That seemed to satisfy them. The topic changed completely and it was only when Cherry was tucked up on the settee that night that she went over those few awkward moments in her mind.

Her parents wouldn't let it rest there. In time they'd give her a push again, a reminder of how young she was, how she'd never planned on being a career girl, how she'd looked forward to marriage and a home of her own and children. Well, that was true. She'd wanted all of those things with David but she didn't, she absolutely did not, want them with anyone else. For her, there was no one else. She was a one-man woman who had lost her man.

He popped into her thoughts again just as she was falling asleep. Not David but Leon Silver. Leon Smith—what a marvellous way of preventing yourself from sleeping—letting thoughts of him trespass into your mind!

Cherry viciously told herself off and turned over on a settee which wasn't half as comfortable to sleep on as it was to sit on. Or was it *him*, robbing her of comfort now just as he did in the office, in a different way?

Leon Silver did just that again on Monday morning, and this time he did it with a vengeance! But this time it wasn't wholly his fault.

Cherry got into work at nine-thirty, there being no need to start early because she was up-to-date, and the next two weeks would be pretty quiet, what with Alec being on holiday. She hung her coat in her office and went to the ladies' room to get water for the flowers she always kept on her desk. Twice a week she bought fresh flowers from an old woman who sat on the steps of a pub near the Underground, selling her wares regardless of the weather.

She was back in the office, arranging golden chrysanthemums in a vase and humming to herself when she became aware that she was being watched. She turned, startled to see Leon Silver in the doorway of Alec's office, his eyes intent upon her.

Cherry's face fell—something which did not go unnoticed by him. 'Good morning, Mr Silver.'

He leaned against the doorjamb, already displeased about something by the look of things. 'Tell me, Mrs Simson, why is it that enchanting smile of yours vanishes every time you set eyes on me?'

'I—don't know what you mean.' She looked away. She wasn't going to rise to that bait, tempting though it was.

'Of course not. Come in here, I want to talk to you.'

About what? Curiosity and a sinking feeling in the pit of her stomach were Cherry's companions as she walked into Alec's office and sat facing Leon Silver. He had been working at Alec's desk, on Alec's projects, that much was obvious from the files and papers she could see.

'I had a phone call from your boss over the week-end. I'm afraid he's met with an accident,' he informed her dispassionately.

'An accident? Oh, no!' Wide eyed, she looked at him in alarm. 'Is it serious?'

'Fairly.' His eyes scanned her face as she sat back with a groan. 'He's fractured his collar bone, broken three ribs, two fingers and a leg . . . just the one leg,' he added drily.

Horrified, Cherry's hands went to her cheeks and she stared at him in disbelief. 'But—but he told me he was good at skiing! He said he was an expert!'

There was an unusual glint in his eyes. 'Oh, it wasn't a skiing accident. He—fell down the steps of the plane when it landed on Saturday morning.'

'What?' She couldn't believe it! And it was unmistakable now, that glint in Leon Silver's eyes. He was amused! 'What—how—what do you mean, he fell down the steps of the plane?'

He gestured with his arm. 'All the way from top . . . to bottom. Or should I say tarmac? That should be clear enough for you. Alec disembarked from the aircraft in a rather—unusual fashion.' The corners of his lips were twitching now. 'I hope he took out plenty of insurance—medical treatment can be expensive in Switzerland.'

He didn't laugh out loud, he managed to restrain himself from doing that but his amusement was obvious. What a bastard! A friend and colleague has a serious accident like this—and Leon Silver is *amused* by it!

Cherry looked down at the carpet, crossed her arms, crossed her legs and thought about the immediate future with a great deal of suspicion.

She might well.

'He'll be laid up for quite a while,' the MD went on, his attitude businesslike again. 'I'll take over as acting Sales Director, and you . . .' The tone of his voice compelled her to look at him. 'And you, Mrs Simson, will carry on as normal.'

As *normal*? Her lips parted in silent protest. Oh, but it was difficult to keep it so! As normal, he'd said! How could she behave normally when she'd be working for a man who unnerved her? And how on earth could he cope with Alec's workload as well as his own?

'So that's that.' He seemed amused again. His smile not only reached his eyes, it also made them glitter but Cherry was too angry, too worried, to notice how attractive they looked. 'Since you obviously have nothing to say, we'll make a start, shall we?'

Nothing to say? Oh, there was so much she wanted to say, but how could she? He was no doubt aware that she didn't want to work for him, just as he was aware that she wouldn't, couldn't, walk out on the company in the throes of an emergency. What choice did she have, really?

He made a point of looking at his watch then. 'Half the morning's gone already, Mrs Simson.' There was a tinge of impatience in his voice now. 'Get the post from Anne's office. She isn't in yet. Bring it in with your post and we'll . . . is something wrong?'

'Well, actually——' She was trying frantically to think of a credible reason why it would be better if he were to borrow a secretary from someone else, why it shouldn't be she who worked for him. There wasn't one. She was secretary to the Sales Director and, for the time being, that was Leon Silver. 'No, nothing's wrong.'

He leaned back in the leather swivel chair, linking both hands behind his head as his eyes moved over her from head to foot. And when he spoke, it was with that air of boredom which infuriated her. 'Mrs Simson, if you aren't capable of coping in an emergency, just say so. But say it *now*.'

There it was again. The challenge. How it would suit him if she were to admit her doubts about her ability to work with him! Or rather, for him. And that was her only doubt, the fact that she would have to spend more time in his presence. She already knew she could cope with the work itself. And his last sentence was a warning, a two-fold warning. She either kept her job or she lost it, she committed herself to his presence for ... for heaven knew how many weeks ... or she didn't. He would not tolerate her giving up half way. That was implicit in his words.

She got to her feet, unconsciously straightening her shoulders. Meeting his gaze levelly, she spoke firmly but not quite as politely as usual. 'I think you'll be surprised to discover what I'm capable of, Mr Silver.' And with that, she left the room, closing the door quietly behind her.

Leon Silver leaned forward and put his hands flat on the surface of the desk, his eyes still fixed on the door. He smiled humourlessly. She was wrong there. He already knew what she was capable of—and it wasn't work he was thinking about.

Penny was busily typing when Cherry went to collect the post. 'I was just wondering whether I should open that myself. I think Mr Silver prefers Anne to do it.'

'I've no doubt he does,' Cherry said sharply. She apologised immediately. Penny was such a nice girl, mousey in colouring and mousey in nature but hardworking and extremely bright. This was only her second job and, she'd said, she would probably stay here for ever. In her innocence she had managed to form a crush on Leon Silver, but give it time, give it time! 'I'm sorry, Penny, I didn't mean to jump down your throat. It's just—have you been told about Mr Moore's accident?'

'What accident?' Anne came in just in time to catch Cherry's last words. 'Good morning, all.' She looked at the post in Cherry's hand. 'I'll take over. Sorry if I panicked you, I wasn't feeling too good when I got up this morning.' She flopped into her chair, shaking her head. 'Ooh, and it's so wretchedly cold! What an effort it was to drag myself here!'

November had just slipped into December but the

weather wasn't all that bad, considering. It obviously was as far as Anne was concerned, though. She looked frozen.

'There's fresh coffee in the pot.' Penny was already moving towards the percolator, having shared Cherry's observation.

'Thanks, Penny. Did I hear you saying Alec has had an accident?'

Cherry nodded but before she could say anything, Anne went on. 'I'm not surprised, you know. All right, he's been taking skiing holidays for years, but it's about time he realised he's fifty-one years old and no longer twenty-nine! For heaven's sake, he spends enough time with his physiotherapist as it is, what with his recurring back trouble—the result of his first skiing accident. I don't know what the man's thinking about!'

Her lack of sympathy was not Cherry's first concern. 'Fifty-one?' she said, incredulous. 'But he looks ten years younger, I've been thinking him ten years younger! Why, I thought he was about the same age as Mr Silver.'

'Do you mind?' Anne seemed to take that as a personal affront. 'Mr Silver is thirty-seven.'

'Oh!' She stuck her hands on her hips. 'Well, he looks older.'

'No, he doesn't. He looks his age. Granted, Alec looks younger than his years but wouldn't we all, if we spent as much time and money on our appearance as he does? I'm not telling you anything you don't know, Cherry. He's vain, let's face it. Anyhow, what's he managed to do to himself?'

It wasn't news to Cherry that Anne didn't care for Alec on a personal level, that the only respect she had for him was regarding his work.

'He didn't hurt himself skiing.' Cherry was irritated by her and she spoke defensively. But it got worse when Anne creased up with laughter on hearing what had happened. She was as bad as Leon Silver. She'd worked

for him for so long that she'd grown to be like him. Or
had he chosen her in the first place because she was like
him—hard and unsympathetic?

'He fell down the steps of the plane!' She creased up
again, repeating the sentence. 'He'd probably been
drinking throughout the journey. Can you see it in your
mind's eye? He's just thanking the stewardess for a
lovely flight and then he takes another one down——'

'If you'll excuse me, I've got other things to do.'
Cherry put the post back on Anne's desk and went into
her own office.

'Good morning, Mrs S. There's a telex for Mr
Moore.'

'Good morning, Danny. Thanks.' She took the telex
from the messenger, a sallow-skinned youth who always
looked at her as though she were a goddess, much to
her amusement, and Alec's.

Her face lit up as she read the message and she
immediately took it in to Leon Silver. 'It's good news!
We've landed the business with Cooper's Beers!'

'Good old Alec! So all his groundwork has paid off
at last.' Smiling, his eyes flicked over the message and
he gave a satisfied nod. 'Here,' he fished in his
waistcoat pocket and took out a small slip of paper.
'This is the phone number of the hospital in
Switzerland. Make a note of it. Get Alec on the
phone—this'll cheer him up . . .'

The day simply sped by and for the most part Cherry
was left alone because Leon Silver had a long meeting
with the Financial Director. Only once was there an
awkward moment, late in the day, when suddenly she
was thrown into a state of nervousness again.

'Having trouble, Mrs Simson?'

The main switchboard had closed down for the night
and the phone had stopped ringing. The fifth floor of
the building was almost deserted, her own office silent,
and this was the time of day when in one hour she
could get though three hours' worth of work. She

almost jumped out of her skin at the sound of Leon's voice, having been concentrating so hard she hadn't heard him come into the room. 'I—er—not really. I haven't quite mastered the art of reading Alec's writing.' She was trying to decipher some handwritten notes he'd left clipped to the file on Cooper's Beers.

'It's quite a knack,' he said quietly. 'I'll grant you that. Let's have a look . . .'

She stiffened as he bent close to her, reading over her shoulder, so close to her that she was aware of the warmth of his body. It made her incredibly nervous for some reason and she kept her eyes riveted to the paper by her typewriter.

Nodding as he interpreted the stream of technical jargon which was her boss's scrawl, terms she was in fact familiar with, it was all she could do not to jerk away from the man whose face was only inches from her own.

'Thank you.' Even her voice didn't come out right! She put her fingers on the home keys of her typewriter and willed him to move away from her.

'You sound tired, Mrs Simson.'

'No, I——' She couldn't move a muscle, kept her eyes on her hands now. Why didn't he go *away*? And why was her heart jumping all over the place? Why was she so nervous of him that this could happen to her against her will?

Suddenly his hand was cupping her chin and he turned her to look at him, his penetrating green eyes probing the depths of violet ones which reflected all the alarm she was feeling. 'I'm perfectly all right, Mr Silver!' She snapped at him. She couldn't help it.

'Then why so afraid? You know, those eyes of yours spend most of their time spitting fire at me. Either that or hatred. But this, this is new. It seems your hatred has turned to fear, and I haven't the faintest idea what I've done to deserve either.'

He still had hold of her, his face so close that she

could feel his breath on her lips. As though her life depended on it, she made a tremendous effort to break the contact of their eyes. He could see too much when he looked at her like that, far too much! It was to be hoped that he was telling the truth, that he could make no sense of her reaction, because she certainly couldn't!

Nor could she bear the touch of his hand any longer. It was strong, firm, cool, yet it felt like fire against her skin. She jerked her head away, striving desperately for nonchalance. 'And I haven't the faintest idea what you're talking about, Mr Silver. I neither hate you nor fear you.'

He straightened, looking down at her from his great height, a ghost of a smile hovering on his lips. 'If you say so. Goodnight, Mrs Simson.'

'Goodnight.' She started typing even before he closed the door and she kept at it until she heard the lift heading for the penthouse. At that instant she stopped, staring stupidly at the gibberish on the paper in the machine. She whipped it out of the roller and flung it in the waste basket.

*Did* she hate him? No, things weren't that bad. And she wasn't afraid of him either, not exactly. It was just ... just that she was so *aware* of him, it made her nervous. She couldn't help feeling that she was on trial, somehow, even though she'd been at Head Office for two months and Alec Moore was obviously satisfied with her.

If only she knew where she stood with Leon Silver, what he thought of her. He had baited her, hadn't he, just now and earlier in the day when he'd broken the news about Alec? She just couldn't shake the feeling that he expected her to pack up and leave at any moment, the feeling that he wanted her to. But that didn't make sense. Come to think of it, there was a great deal about him which didn't make sense.

She pulled on her coat, frowning. There were several things about her which didn't make sense, either—like

the effect his nearness had on her. It was probably just
the sheer size of the man. His physical nearness
probably made most people feel threatened.

Didn't it?

It was only as she was getting ready for bed that
night that she allowed herself a smile about Alec's
tumble. Knowing him, he'd probably been flirting with
the stewardess rather than thanking her. Something
must have caused him to miss his step! Poor Alec, he
would miss the office party the week before Christmas.
Even if he were fit enough to fly back to England by
then, he'd probably not be able to attend. The party
was for the entire staff of Head Office and would be
held in the dining rooms and, according to Anne,
whose job it was to organise things with the catering
manageress, it was always an enjoyable affair . . .

Which led to another thought, a worrying thought
which managed to bring Leon Silver back into her mind
and keep her awake for an hour. There had been some
invitations in the post that day, some from suppliers
and a couple from customers. They were for various
Christmas functions, cocktail parties, luncheons and so
on, and she had been told by the MD which ones to
accept. 'Ring round and let these people know that Alec
won't be available, but I'll be attending,' he'd said,
informing her that he'd received similar invitations in
his own post. 'And you'd better prepare yourself for the
rounds, Mrs Simson.'

'I'm sorry?'

'Christmas get-togethers.' He'd shrugged, tapping the
invitation cards as he dropped them on her desk.
'You'll be coming with me.'

'Me? But—surely this has nothing to do with business?'

'It has everything to do with business.' His reply was
brusque. 'And if Alec were here, you'd be going with
him. As it is, you'll be going with me . . . Kindly take
that look off your face, Mrs Simson. Duty calls, so
you'll have to grin and bear it.'

She would, of course. But she wasn't looking forward to it one little bit. She might not hate Leon Silver but she certainly didn't like the man, either, and there was no way she would ever feel at ease in his company—in or out of the office.

# CHAPTER FIVE

'I DON'T really know how to answer that one, Daddy.'
Cherry smiled, glancing appreciatively around the
subtly-lit restaurant. She was in luxurious surroundings
and if she'd known her father intended to bring her to
such an expensive place, she'd have taken a change of
clothes to work with her. He'd been in London all day,
at a seminar, and had phoned to say he'd take her out
to dinner before driving back to Bristol.

He'd picked her up from work an hour ago and had
just asked her how she was getting along with her
temporary boss. 'Last week he gave me hell, deliberately
made life difficult for me—or so it seemed. It was, have
you done this, have you done that? "Mrs Simson,
what's happened to my phone call to Nairobi? Where's
the coffee I asked you for ten minutes ago? You must
learn to delegate, Mrs Simson. Leave yourself free to
attend to my needs. You should be one step ahead of
me. I suggest you shape up or give up!"'

She tucked into her beautifully presented hors
d'oeuvre and glanced helplessly at her father. 'But this
week, it's been so different! He hasn't been on my back
at all, and this morning, would you believe, he even
said, "Well done." Twice! How about that?'

Michael Marshall gave his daughter an indulgent smile.
She might not care for the enigmatic Leon Silver but
working with him had certainly given her something to
think about, had brought to her lovely face a vivacity and
animation he hadn't seen for a long time. So, whatever Mr
Silver was or was not, Michael was grateful to the man. 'I
don't see why you're so puzzled, darling. It seems to me
that last week Mr Silver had to spend time knocking you
into shape. You know, training you to his way of working.'

'No, Daddy! It's nothing so simple. Nothing about him can be easily fathomed.'

'Then how do you explain the difference in his behaviour last week and his behaviour this week?'

'I can't.'

'Why didn't you have a chat with his own secretary? Last week, I mean. Perhaps she'd have given you a few pointers about him.'

'I don't really chat to Anne at all. Firstly, there's not time—we've only ever had lunch together once. And secondly she's a bit aloof, you see. She does a lot of Mr Silver's private and personal work—like organising dinner parties, for instance, and I think she considers herself a bit superior because of it, though I don't know why she should. And she never says a word about him except to sing his praises... Mind you,' she added, forgetting the food in front of her, 'even I have to admit he's extremely well organised. For two weeks he's coped with Alec's work as well as his own! He's dynamic, indefatigable. And his door's always open to people. He's a trouble-shooter, a superb Director; provided he isn't in a meeting, anyone can go in to see him anytime. He told me from the start that it was no part of my job to try to keep people away from him...

'He's a qualified architect, did I tell you that? And he's an engineer...' She broke off, shaking her head, amused by the memory of something which had happened the day before.

On Wednesday morning she had got in early, as usual, and she'd found Leon kneeling on the floor in Anne's office—surrounding by pieces of photocopying machine! She had stopped in her tracks, her eyes going to his filthy hands. 'Mr Silver! What on earth are you doing?'

'Good morning, Mrs Simson. How many guesses would you like?'

'But—but why didn't you send for the engineer? I'll ring——'

'It's too early. Besides, I'm enjoying myself.'

'You are?'

'I am.' He started putting bits and pieces together again. 'But I'd like to know who was the last person to use this thing last night.'

'Not I!' She perched on the side of a desk, arms folded as she watched in fascination. It was just so—so incongruous, seeing the expensively dressed Chairman of the company fixing a photocopying machine!

He muttered something about the cleaners and their tampering. 'The cleaners? Oh, I don't think so, Mr Silver. They don't clean the office equipment.'

'I didn't mean they've been cleaning it, I meant they've been using it.'

He turned to look at her then, a rueful smile touching his mouth. 'Knitting patterns—the copying of. Don't look so surprised. Every job has its own little perks, mm? I've caught the office cleaners copying recipes and knitting patterns more than once!' He'd started laughing then, outrageous, rumbling laughter which communicated itself to Cherry. Was there nothing going on in this building that he didn't know about? It certainly looked that way!

Michael Marshall put down his knife and fork, satisfied with his first course and very satisfied to see his daughter laughing like this. Was that a hint of admiration he could see in her eyes? For the mysterious Mr Silver? The man she had spent so much time angrily raving about only a few weeks ago? 'And did the photocopier work when he'd put it back together again?'

'Of course!'

'Well, I'm very glad to hear you're getting on so well now.'

Cherry sobered at once. 'Daddy, I didn't say that! I don't like the man, make no mistake. But he's—just more tolerable these days, that's all.'

But that wasn't all. Not quite. A strange thing had

happened today. Leon had been at the factory in Southampton, had been absent all day and—and the place had been almost dull without him. That is, even though she was madly busy she had ... had sort of missed him. It was too ridiculous, really, when she should have been enjoying the comparative peace his absence represented.

As she tucked into her main course, she wondered about that. The feeling had been short-lived, had come to her late in the day when suddenly she had wondered why the day seemed so routine, lacking the sparkle of other days.

'... and heard on the radio fog's forecast for tonight.'

She looked up. All the time her father had been chatting, half her mind had been on Leon Silver. Bother the man. Why did he have to haunt her out of office hours?

'Why don't you stay with me tonight and drive home in the——' She stopped dead, her eyes dropping instantly to the plate in front of her. Leon Silver had just come into the restaurant—in the flesh!

'I can't,' her father was saying. 'It's Friday tomorrow and I've got patients from nine o'clock onwards, as usual. But thanks for the offer, darling ... What's wrong? What are you thinking about?'

'Nothing. I—don't look now, Daddy, but Mr Silver's just walked in.' And he had a beautiful woman on his arm, a very tall blonde who was wearing a green silk dress and an expression of total confidence. She was not the clinging type, she stood proud, statuesque, giving the impression that she knew exactly who she was and where she belonged—with the man who was smiling down at her.

A tremor of nervousness ran through Cherry. That and a vague feeling of ... of something she couldn't put a name to. She was bound to be spotted by him, and she didn't want to be. Oh, why did her father have to bring her here, why did he have to treat her to somewhere really expensive?

Pull yourself together, you ungracious fool. She told herself off sternly, relieved to see that Leon and the blonde had been shown to a corner table and that she had not been spotted. Their table was diagonally across the room from herself and her father—about as far away from them as possible. But all she wanted to do now was to get out of there. Of course she couldn't. The waiter was approaching with a trolley of delicious desserts and there was no way she'd hurt her father's feelings by hurrying him up. Nor would she let him know how much Leon Silver's presence affected her now, just as it always did.

'What a difficult choice!' She smiled as her father gave his order, her eyes on the temptations on the trolley. 'I shouldn't, but I'm going to have the profiteroles—with lashings of cream.'

'And why not?' Leon Silver's voice held amusement. It also had the power to send a shiver down her spine. She looked up to find that his eyes were on her, moving appreciatively from her face to the pretty lace blouse she was wearing—and back to her face. 'You have no need to count the calories.' He inclined his head, bowing slightly. 'Good evening, Mrs Simson.'

The waiter withdrew, leaving Cherry with a plate of food she no longer wanted. 'Why, Mr Silver. How nice! How was your day in Southampton?' How she managed to appear so cool, she didn't know. Nor did she know why that familiar nervousness had taken hold of her. 'Er—may I introduce Michael Marshall, my father? Daddy, this is Leon Silver, our Chairman.'

'Ah, yes.' Cherry's father did not let her down. He was super. As if Leon Silver's name merely rang a bell, he said, 'Cherry has mentioned you to me. How do you do, Mr Silver?'

'Mr—Marshall? Oh, but of course!' Leon's smile was a real one. 'I tend to forget that your daughter was once married.' His eyes moved from the older man to Cherry—and locked momentarily with hers before flitting briefly to the rings on her wedding finger. 'And what brings you to London, Mr Marshall? You're a dentist, I believe.'

'That's right. I've been attending a seminar. And very interesting it was, too.'

'I don't remember telling you that, Mr Silver—that my father's a dentist.'

He leaned fractionally closer. 'You didn't. Well, if you'll excuse me, there's someone waiting for me. I hope to meet you again sometime, Mr Marshall.'

Cherry couldn't resist the temptation. As the big man walked away she turned and stole a glance at the woman who was waiting for him. She was reading a menu, paying no attention to the people her escort had been saying hello to.

'Well, what a turn up!' Her father's voice was enthusiastic. 'You never mentioned that he's so young! I'd envisaged someone much older. You never told me he's handsome, either!'

Taken aback by the ring of accusation in his last sentence, Cherry shrugged her slender shoulders. 'I thought I'd told you he's thirty-seven. You can hardly call that young, Daddy. He's only sixteen years younger than you!'

'Thanks very much.'

She giggled. 'Sorry. That didn't sound right, did it? Anyway, I don't happen to think of him as young—or handsome. He's . . . vaguely attractive, I suppose.'

'There's nothing vague about him, and you know it.'

She changed the subject at once. How right her father was! Not in any respect could Leon Silver be described as vague. He had that certain something which drew attention whether he wanted it or not. It was far more than his stature which made him impossible to ignore; he had charisma. Even her father had been captured by it.

It was just as well that Michael wanted to get back to Bristol because it enabled Cherry to have an early night. He dropped her off at her house and refused her offer of coffee. She gave him a kiss and thanked him for a lovely meal, promising to ring her mother at the week-end.

She got up earlier than usual on the Friday, anticipating an unusually busy day. Anne was going to the ante-natal clinic and was taking the whole day off because Leon Silver was leaving for a cocktail party at three—and Cherry was going with him. Until then, she'd be taking over in Anne's office and Penny Davies would work at Cherry's desk.

Leon emerged from his office as soon as Cherry got in, before she had a chance to hang the dress she'd taken to work with her. 'Good morning, Mrs Simson . . . Is that what you're wearing to the shindig this afternoon?'

'Yes.' She shook the dress out and hung it neatly on a hanger. It was, appropriately, a cocktail dress, knee-length with a V neck and tightly fitting sleeves. It was made from black jersey which had a shiny thread running through it and it was, she thought, just right. But something in Leon Silver's voice put a doubt in her mind. 'You don't think it's—appropriate?'

She turned to look at him. He was sitting on the typing chair, his feet stuck on the edge of Anne's desk. As usual he was minus his jacket, his humbs hooked into the pockets of a snugly-fitting waistcoat which showed off his physique. His broad shoulders lifted in a shrug. 'Do you care what I think?'

'Yes, actually. If you don't think it's appropriate, I'll——'

'The style's appropriate. But you wear too much black for my liking. One could be forgiven for thinking you're still in mourning.'

Cherry clamped her lips together, angered as much by his words as the over-casual way in which he spoke them.

'How long is it since your husband died, Mrs Simson?'

'Almost four years,' she said stiffly. She turned her back on him and fiddled with the dress. 'But I happen to think that black is my colour. I'm told it suits me.'

'By whom?'

'By various people.' He was annoying her and she couldn't really figure out why.

'I was surprised when I saw you in the restaurant last night,' he went on. She thought he'd changed the subject but she was wrong. 'Interesting, I thought when I saw you, Cherry Simson has a preference for older men.'

'Is that what you thought?' She turned to look at him, her eyes spitting fire again. 'And then you discovered it was my father.'

'So I did.' A slow smile started, a slow and infuriating smile which put green lights in his eyes. 'So tell me, what sort of men do you prefer, Mrs Simson?'

She realised what it was then, that which was annoying her. It was the way he was using her name—often and with an unusual emphasis. 'None, Mr Silver. None at all.'

'Indeed?' The word came lazily, curiously, making her realise that he had extracted from her more than she had intended to let him know. 'So you are still mourning your husband.'

Unconsciously, Cherry's hands went to her hips in an attitude of aggression. She never talked to strangers about David and she wasn't going to start now. What went on in her mind and her heart was nobody's business but hers. 'Mr Silver, I have a great deal to do this morning.'

He said nothing. He just looked at her, letting his eyes roam slowly over her face and down the length of her body until they came to rest on her hips. She dropped her hands, dispensing with the aggression in the pose she'd adopted, and up came his eyes, full of amusement now. 'That's better,' he said, in a voice which was dangerously soft. He got slowly to his feet, his eyes not leaving her for one instant. 'And now if you'll excuse me, I too have a great deal to do.'

For several seconds Cherry stood looking at the closed door to his office. What on earth was that all about? And why hadn't she stood her ground? With one look he had managed to tell her off for her attitude towards him—and she'd taken it! Why hadn't she told him that what he'd asked her had nothing to do with business and was therefore nothing to do with him?

Maybe she was being silly, but the incident managed to annoy her all morning. And what a morning it was! Penny's mother telephoned to say that her daughter had a streaming cold and wouldn't be coming in, so Cherry had to get on to Personnel and ask for someone to be sent from the typing pool. She then had to spend half an hour with the girl, explaining things to her, and in between all this the telephone rang with its usual frequency, she had to hunt for a file which had gone missing, and Leon Silver demanded to know why she wasn't at her desk when he buzzed for her!

By twelve o'clock, however, everything was under control and Cherry had dealt with most of the things that particularly needed to be dealt with. She was at her desk, debating whether or not to take half an hour off for lunch, when the outer door opened and a most unlikely visitor walked in.

It was an old lady carrying several shopping bags, a very old lady, someone Cherry had never seen before. She was wearing a full-length sable coat and, incredibly, on her head a battered red woollen hat. To say that the hat and coat laughed at each other would be an understatement and the impression of eccentricity was added to by the black plastic overshoes on the ends of very thin legs in a pair of lisle stockings.

Cherry's eyebrows rose, but only slightly, and on her face there was a polite smile. She greeted the visitor as she would greet any other visitor, having realised several things at once. The receptionist on the ground floor had not rung to announce the old lady's arrival, the fur cost she was wearing was genuine, as were the diamonds on her fingers, and she hadn't bothered to knock before opening the office door. This was someone who knew her way around, someone Cherry ought to recognise. But she didn't.

'Good afternoon. May I help you?'

'My dear, you must be Cherry Simson? How nice!' The soft, cultured voice was another surprise. Had Cherry spoken to this lady over the telephone, she'd have taken her for many years younger than she actually was. She was probably eighty years old, judging by the crinkled skin on her hands and face, but she had once been lovely, if not beautiful. Her features told of this and her light blue eyes spoke of a curiosity and a zest for life which had not been diminished by the years.

Cherry liked her at once. Her smile changed to laughter and she held out her hand as the old lady approached. 'I am. And you are. . . .?'

'And where is the mother-to-be?' They'd spoken simultaneously. 'I was hoping to congratulate her personally. I'll sit down here, my dear. Is there anyone in with him? Is that coffee hot? I say, what a pretty blouse! Black's certainly your colour, isn't it?'

Cherry suppressed a smile, thinking her adorable. 'Thank you.' She dealt with one question at a time, as curious as anything, wondering how this person managed to look so small and lost when she was so acutely observant! She was painfully thin, and Cherry towered over her by at least six inches, two of which were the heels on her shoes. 'Anne's gone to the ante-natal clinic today. She won't be back, I'm afraid. Mr Silver is just along the corridor, in the finance department. He won't be long. Er—who shall I say wants to see him?'

'Oh! I'm his grandmother. Didn't I say? No, well, I don't often come into London,' she went on, as if that would explain the omission. 'I'm Leon's paternal grandmother, Helena Silver. It would have been better without the "a", wouldn't it? Just Helen, then it would flow better when you put the two names together.'

It was more than Cherry could do to suppress her smile at that. Laughter bubbled out of her as she silently went over the name, Helena Silver. 'Yes, I see your point, though it has a certain rhythm as it is. Mrs Silver, would you like a cup of coffee? It's nice and hot.'

The old lady sat back and cuddled her coat around her. 'Oh, no thank you! I never touch the stuff!'

'Er—oh. Well, how about a cup of tea?'

'It is Cherry, isn't it? What a lovely name! Well, Cherry, it's a little too cold for tea, wouldn't you say?' She said it so seriously that Cherry had to bite hard into her cheeks.

'Then what can I get you?'

'A nice drop of whisky. Some of that very old stuff Leon keeps in his cabinet in there.'

Cherry fetched the bottle and a glass. There was only one sure way of getting this right. 'Say "when", Mrs Silver.'

'. . . When. And is there any hot water in your kettle? And a spoonful of sugar, perhaps? You wouldn't have a slice of lemon, would you?'

Grinning like a Cheshire cat, the younger woman shook her head. 'Not in here, but I can send down for some——'

'No, no. This will be fine. I don't want to put——'

The door swung open and Leon Silver walked in, his black eyebrows shooting up in astonishment. 'Grannie!' he boomed, seeming more amazed than pleased. 'What the devil are you doing in town? And why are you wearing that awful hat? Isn't it time you threw that away? It doesn't do a thing for you.'

The old lady didn't bat an eye. 'Yes it does. It keeps

my head warm. Good day, Leon. I'm drinking your whisky and talking to Cherry. You didn't tell me what a pretty girl she is.'

'No, well—I don't tell you everything, do I?' His eyes were dancing with laughter . . . and love.

Something inside Cherry Simson melted and sent a feeling of tenderness surging through her. She looked in fascination at Leon Silver's eyes and forgot completely his hardness, his sarcasm, all the negative things about him. What a picture this made, this giant of a man and this little old lady, now chipping at one another as though they were enemies—and loving every minute of it.

'The twins are on school holidays, that's why I'm here.'

'Grannie, I'm well aware that my children are on holiday! Now don't do your batty act with me, what's their being on holiday got to do with you're being in town?'

'I brought them to see Father Christmas.'

'They don't believe in that old gentleman. Good grief!' he bellowed suddenly, startling his secretary if not his grandmother. 'You didn't drive here, did you? Not with my children in the car!'

'Don't be silly, Leon, I haven't driven for twenty years.'

'Grannie! You wrote-off one of my father's cars only two years ago.'

'Yes, well, there was that one occasion . . . don't boom at me like that! Does he bully you, Cherry?'

'Yes.' She didn't look at him.

'And is he as rude to you as he is to me?'

'Yes.'

She heard Leon's intake of breath and bit into her cheeks again. She could feel his eyes boring into her but she wouldn't look at him.

'You'd better be careful, Leon. Cherry is Piscean, you must learn to be gentle with her if you're to get on well with her.'

They both looked at her, Cherry in astonishment and Leon with disdain.

'Aw, Grannie! Don't start. Please!'

'But Mrs Silver—how on earth did you know I'm a Pisces?'

'Mrs Simson!' Leon's voice cracked like a whip. 'Don't set her off. She just knows these things, heaven help us, and I don't want her filling your head with all that—*Grannie!*' He interrupted himself, his hands going up in an attitude of despair. 'If you brought the children to see Father Christmas, *where are they now?*'

Helena Silver took a little sip of her warm whisky and shrugged. 'Didn't I say, dear? They're riding up and down in the lift. You know how they enjoy——'

'Oh, for heaven's sake!' Leon looked towards the ceiling. 'Cherry, go and retrieve them at once!'

She did. She walked down the corridor in a state of utter confusion, torn between anger and laughter. He had called her Cherry for the first time ever but he had spoken to her as if she were a dog! 'Go and retrieve them at once!'

His grandmother's visit was something they could well do without on this particular day—oh, but she was a delight!

She pressed the lift button, giggling and irritated at the same time. If she had known Leon had a grandmother, she'd never have imagined he would call her 'Grannie'. It just sounded so odd coming from him!

The lift doors opened and Cherry stuck her foot against one of them, her face breaking into a smile. 'Have either of you been seasick?'

Two heads shook in unison and two pairs of eyes looked at her with uncertainty. Oh Lord, she said to herself, what have we here? Two pairs of eyes were watching her, eyes so very, very much like their father's ... and yet so different. These eyes had not yet discovered how to hide the thoughts behind them, had not yet learned what cynicism meant, had not lived long enough to reflect the world-weariness sometimes noticeable in Leon's eyes. Yet how similar they were, how green, how dark the lashes that framed them!

Their mother must have been very pretty indeed ... and that was all Cherry had time to register.

'Did Daddy send you to fetch us?'

'Is he cross? He isn't cross, is he?'

'Are you his new secretary?'

She let out a long sigh, bemused by the twins' identical faces, bemused by their questions, the morning she'd had, the answer she should give them. 'I'm your father's ...' She crossed her arms resignedly and leaned against the door as it tried to close. '... dogsbody.'

'Dogsbody?'

'What's a dogsbody?'

She regretted what she'd said instantly. Two faces were frowning, interested, entertained by a word they didn't know the meaning of. They weren't going to let this drop, she just knew it! 'Forget all about it, girls. All it means is that I'm a very busy lady, so come along. Your father wants you.'

One of them groaned and stepped out of the lift. The other hung back. '*Is* he cross?'

Cherry didn't know the answer to that until she presented Leon with his children. He was at his desk, there was no sign of Grannie, and he was scribbling on a pad in front of him.

'Your children, Mr Silver.'

He looked up, frowning at them. 'Good afternoon, you two. No more riding in the lift without my permission—which will not be granted during office hours. Understood?' He didn't wait for an answer, he took it as read. 'Now then, have you introduced yourselves to Mrs Simson?'

It happened again, the heads shaking in unison.

'Very well.' Leon got to his feet. 'Mrs Simson, this is Rachael and this is Veronica, otherwise known as Ronnie. Rachael, Ronnie, shake hands with Mrs Simson.'

They did so, and Rachael said, 'You've got very pretty eyes, Mrs Simson.'

'We don't make personal remarks to people we're only just meeting,' their father informed them. 'Sit down, children. As soon as Grannie reappears, we'll go upstairs and have some lunch. I suppose it was your idea to come into London by train, Rachael?' He turned to Cherry. 'For some obscure reason, my children like riding in lifts, trains and taxis.'

'And escalators, Daddy!'

'Oh yes, and escalators.'

Cherry smiled. Rachael, she'd noted, was the more outgoing of the two. It was just as well they were wearing different clothes or she'd have had trouble remembering which was which. The night watchman had been right when he'd said they were identical. She went back to her own office and carried on as best she could, hoping that the rest of the day would not be as chaotic as the morning had been.

When Mrs Silver came back a few minutes later, she and the twins were ushered out of the office by Leon. 'Mrs Simson, I'll have lunch upstairs with my family. Ring Mrs Morrison and ask her to organise it, will you? Tell her to send whatever's on the menu and that the girls will have ice-cream for afters. Buzz O'Connell first and tell him we're on our way up.'

'Won't you join us, Cherry?' The question came from Mrs Silver, and Cherry looked at her boss, feeling awkward, unsure how to answer.

He nodded. 'We'd be delighted.'

But he didn't look as though he meant it. 'Thank you, but no. I have a few things to finish off before we leave for Croydon.'

'Don't worry about that. Anything that isn't done can wait till Monday. Did Anne leave her keys with you?'

He was referring to the key which one needed to take the lift beyond the fifth floor and the key to the penthouse. She nodded. 'Good. Then please join us when you've made your calls. Tell the switchboard where we are so they can put any urgent calls through upstairs. And bring that,' he added, pointing to her dress. 'You might as well change upstairs and make use of the bathroom.'

There were in fact two bathrooms in the penthouse. Three, probably—assuming there was one en suite to the master bedroom. Cherry was shown to a guest room by Leon's chauffeur-cum-butler, Graham O'Connell, and in there she left her change of clothing and her vanity case. It was the first time she'd been into the apartment, and it was both luxurious and vast, covering most of the floor of the building and comprising four guest bedrooms, a study, a games room in which there was a full-size snooker table, and a sparklingly clean fitted kitchen-cum-breakfast room which had in it every piece of labour-saving equipment one could think of. It was O'Connell who gave her the guided tour, at Leon's request, and O'Connell who served the lunch which was delivered by one of the waitresses from the dining room downstairs.

'Grannie, it's two o'clock.' Leon checked his watch, explaining to his grandmother that he and Cherry were leaving for Croydon at three. 'Would you like O'Connell to take you to the station or have you more shopping to do?'

'You can leave us to our own devices, thank you.' The old lady looked at the twins, her eyes full of mischief. 'We have one or two things to buy and then we'll take a taxi to the station.'

'And one at the other end,' Rachael put in. 'You won't let Maxwell come and pick us up, will you, Grannie?'

'Well, that will depend on how tired we are. We'll see.'

'And bear that in mind, you two,' Leon warned. 'You are not to tire Grannie.'

'Yes, Daddy.' They were gathering their shopping together.

Cherry had been shown their presents from Father Christmas, and she got to her feet now. 'Well, I think it's time I got changed. It was lovely meeting you, children. Have fun this afternoon.'

'We will see you again, won't we, Mrs Simson?' It was Ronnie who asked this, accompanied by enthusiastic nods from Rachael, and it was Mrs Silver who answered the question.

'Yes, of course you will. My dear,' she smiled, turning to Cherry with a thin hand outstretched, 'I've so enjoyed meeting you, and thank you for looking after me earlier.' Her light blue eyes flicked swiftly to Leon, who was helping the girls into their coats. 'And be warned,' she added in a stage-whisper, planting an unexpected kiss on Cherry's cheek, 'his bite is just as bad as his bark. He's a Scorpio, you know. He'll learn all your secrets and——'

'Grannie, what are you whispering about?'

'Nothing, Leon! I was just saying goodbye to Cherry.'

Leon ushered his family to the door and Cherry went to get changed. She took a quick shower, too, and was grateful for the opportunity. She was also glad she'd had something to eat. It would not have been wise to attend a cocktail party without having eaten something first.

She emerged at ten minutes to three, knowing that her boss intended to leave at three, and he joined her in the living room at five minutes to, having changed into a light grey suit which was teamed with a white silk shirt and the usual matching waistcoast. Savile Row! Leon's clothes were conservative, immaculate, and had quality written all over them. He looked impeccable and extremely attractive.

He said nothing at all about Cherry's appearance but his eyes did not reflect disapproval as they swept slowly over the black dress which hugged her figure in all the right places. Nor had her confidence been shaken by his earlier remarks. As soon as she'd put on fresh make-up and finished restyling her hair in a softly coiled chignon, leaving a few wisps of curls to frame her face, she had examined her reflection in the mirror. At her throat she had a slim, plain gold necklace, with small, matching earrings, and apart from the rings on her wedding finger, that was all the jewellery she had on. That was all the jewellery she needed. She looked good, and she knew it.

Nevertheless that awful nervousness took hold of her as she underwent Leon's scrutiny. He crossed over to her and took the jacket she was holding. 'Allow me.' He held it open for her and she slipped her arms into it. 'I've told O'Connell to bring the car round to the main entrance,' he said, his deep voice quiet as he stood too close for comfort behind her. For just a moment his hands came to rest on her shoulders and then he moved away. 'If you're ready, Mrs Simson . . .'

It got worse as she stopped into the lift with him. It wasn't a small lift, but with him inside it she always felt as though it were and she started chattering in the hope of distracting herself. 'Are the twins staying with your grandmother while they're on holiday?'

'Yes, at the family house in Bucks. She lives with my father and stepmother.'

'She's an amazing lady. She must be—what? Eighty years old?' She kept her eyes on the illuminated panel over the doors, watching as they moved from the penthouse and past the fifth floor.

'Eighty-four, actually. Amazing isn't the right word. She's wildly eccentric . . .'

The fourth floor.

'She can also be quite deaf when she chooses to be, but don't be fooled. She's also . . .'

The third floor.

'. . . as sharp as a razor, although she tries——'

The lift stopped.

Cherry gasped in horror. At some point between the third and second floor, the lift stopped dead and the lights went off. She went rigid with fear. Never in her life had she been trapped in a lift, and all her life she had feared it might one day happen. But she had never really believed it would, not to her. These things always happened to someone else, so while she didn't like using lifts, she'd never avoided them.

'Oh, God, no!' Without even thinking about it, she reached out in the darkness to touch her companion. *'Leon!'*

'Hey, take it easy!' An arm came firmly around her shoulders. 'We'll be racing again in a moment. It's just a power-cut, not to worry.'

'A power-cut!' Cherry's handbag dropped to the floor and she started trembling from head to toe. She had visions of the lift cable snapping at any second and their plummeting to the basement. It was pitch black; there was no light from the panel, no sound from outside, nothing.

The arm around her shoulders tightened, and she leaned against the warm wall that was his chest. 'Good grief, you're shaking!'

'I can't help it, I can't help it! I'm *terrified*!'

'Now listen to me...' Leon spoke to her very quietly, very firmly, his lips almost touching her hair as he explained that they were perfectly safe, that the lights would come on and the lift would be in motion in a matter of minutes, that people were working right now to correct whatever had gone wrong.

It didn't help. 'I can't stand it!' Cherry could hardly get her voice out, she was so frightened. 'Being suspended in mid-air like this, I can't stand it!'

'My dear girl, we're not dangling on a piece of cotton!' This time he gave her a technical explanation, something about cables and counter-balances, but Cherry just shook in her shoes.

'Oh, for heaven's sake, woman——' He pulled her closer, enveloping her with one arm against his body. His free hand moved to the back of her head and suddenly he was kissing her.

There was a split second delay while Cherry's brain assimilated what was happening as she was pulled against him, and by the time his mouth claimed hers, she was fighting him, her whereabouts completely forgotten. 'What the—*Stop* that!' She wrenched her head away, her hands moving up to push against his chest.

'Shut up!' His voice was a command, his breath cool and fresh against her mouth. The hand at the back of her head became firmer and the arm around her body became a vice. She was kissed with a ruthlessness which drove all fear of the darkness from her mind and replaced it with a new fear.

To struggle against Leon Silver was futile. It also became less and less desirable as his mouth moved against hers, parting her lips until he was kissing her with an intimacy which caused her to tremble all over again. It seemed that all the strength in her body drained from her fingertips, her toes. There was an instant when he lifted his head—only to move his lips to her neck, to cover the soft, perfumed skin with little, explorative kisses before meeting once again with her mouth.

And it was a meeting. She was kissing him back because it was too good, too delicious to be denied. Her arms moved around him, holding him closer so the entire length of her body was against him.

The sudden flickering of lights was a shocking intrusion.

He let go of her, looking down at her with eyes which were hooded, showing not the slightest trace of emotion, telling her nothing at all as the lift continued its descent.

Her cheeks flaming under his gaze, his nonchalance,

Cherry stared at him with accusation in her eyes. 'And what was that in aid of?'

One dark brow rose sardonically. 'My dear Mrs Simson, I should have thought it obvious.' He shrugged, stepping aside as the lift opened on the ground floor. 'I had to think of something which would counteract your hysteria.'

Cherry was silent for a long time on the drive to Croydon. She was shaken, and it had nothing to do with her being trapped in the lift. She and Leon were in the back seat of the black Rolls Royce and though there was a panel of glass separating them from the driver, they had no need for privacy. Nothing was said for a long time. She kept her eyes on the passing scenery as they wound their way from London to Surrey, feeling acutely self-conscious and foolish.

Leon's kiss had resurrected in her something which had died long ago, something which had died when David died. Confusion and guilt had descended on her like a damp fog. She knew, now, why Leon Silver's presence affected her the way it did. She was attracted to him physically. Had such ideas not been so alien to her thinking, she'd have realised it before. Weeks ago. She was physically attracted to him and she didn't want to be. It felt like . . . like a betrayal of David, and telling herself that David was gone forever did not lessen her sense of guilt.

Quite apart from that, there was the certain knowledge that the man beside her had felt nothing, nothing at all. He had kissed her merely as a means of distracting her from her fear, and it had worked. To him, that was all there was to it, and it made her feel foolish for returning his kiss, for responding to what had been nothing more than a clever tactic.

'Mrs Simson, are we to make this entire journey in silence? If you can tear yourself away from scenery you must have seen a hundred times before, I'd like to talk to you about next week.'

She turned to look at him, her expression impassive. 'You have my full attention, Mr Silver.'

'Really?' he drawled. He looked positively annoyed. 'Why don't you spit it out, whatever it is you want to say? Don't sit there with those big blue eyes shooting flames at me.'

She wasn't aware that they were. 'There's nothing I want to—spit out,' she said coolly, letting him know she disliked the expression. 'You were saying, about next week?'

'I spoke to the Managing Director of Cooper's Beers this morning, about their new brewery. They are using that firm of architects I recommended in Nairobi, it's a subsidiary of a British company who have a great deal of experience of building in Kenya. Anyway, we're having lunch with Cooper's on Tuesday and there'll be a meeting which will go on all afternoon, probably. Wednesday is the office party, as you know, and Thursday—are you free on Thursday evening? Anne has arranged a dinner party for me in the penthouse and I'd like you to act as hostess.'

'Is it concerned with business?'

She saw his face tighten and instantly regretted her words, even though the answer mattered very much to her. If this were merely a social occasion, she'd just as soon not be present. Besides, he could get the statuesque blonde to act as hostess; he wouldn't need her. Come to think of it, he could no doubt call on a dozen women to act as his hostess, a man such as he. She sighed inwardly. She needn't have asked the question, had she thought about it first . . .

Which was just what Leon Silver pointed out. 'Mrs Simson, don't you think I've already got the message that there's no way you wish to subject yourself to my company if it has nothing to do with your job? You made that quite clear when I told you to prepare yourself for the Christmas get-togethers, and again today when you were reluctant to have lunch in my apartment. So if you have a date on Thursday—which I very much doubt—cancel it. You are needed to act as hostess to some *business* acquaintances—six in all. Three men, two wives and one mistress. All right?'

She should have known better than to say any more. If it hadn't been such a traumatic day one way and another, she would probably have been thinking more clearly. But she didn't and she wasn't. 'Yes, it's all right. But who did this sort of thing for you in the past? I mean——'

'In the past,' he said harshly, 'my wife. My wife, Mrs Simson. But my wife died almost six years ago—in case you didn't know. Since then my secretary has often acted as hostess to dinner parties which involve business colleagues. And before you ask, Anne has already made it clear to me that her current "inelegance" precludes her from this particular task. Personally I think she's looking quite radiant, but there you are. There's also the fact that her husband is anxious that she doesn't do too much at the moment. I had a chat to him on the telephone only last week and, like me, he'd rather Anne stopped working now.'

'But—I thought it was you who was urging Anne to stay on till the last minute?'

'She is staying on till the last minute—but not through my urging. She wants to, and since she's been with me for fourteen years I can hardly throw her out, can I? I'll be damned lucky to find a replacement who's as loyal and conscientious as Anne,' he added pointedly. 'However, since you are neither pregnant nor married to someone—anxious or otherwise—can you bring yourself to share my company for business reasons next Thursday?'

Cherry gave him her sweetest smile, hating him for his sarcasm. 'Why, Mr Silver, I'd be delighted.'

'Like hell!'

'Is there any chance of my taking Friday morning off? I know it's our last working day but I'd planned on

going late night shopping on Thursday, and
Christmas——'

'Take the whole day off, Mrs Simson, take the whole
day!' And with that, he turned to watch the passing
scenery.

His mood did not improve. Several hours later
Cherry was dropped off outside her home with a
perfunctory 'Goodnight, Mrs Simson.' He did not wish
her a good week-end, nor did he make any comment
about the party they'd attended.

It had not been the first cocktail party Cherry had
been to and she knew the drill. One did not sit down,
one circulated and chatted, glass in hand, and ate if one
were so inclined the delicious little tit-bits which were
brought round on trays.

As it was, she went into her kitchen undecided whether
to cook a meal for herself or not. She settled for a
sandwich and curled up in an armchair by the fire,
feeling dissatisfied and miserable. Leon had introduced
her to several people at the party and in time they had
become separated, talking in different groups. From a
distance she had seen him laughing, apparently enjoying
himself, but as soon as they got into the car, he'd
slipped back into the dark mood which had descended
on him after their conversation on the journey there.

The journey back to London had been silent except
for the two attempts Cherry had made at conversation.
These had been met with little more than grunts. It was
her fault, she couldn't deny that it was her fault. She
had irritated the hell out of him by appearing reluctant
to act as his hostess next week and all the headway
she'd recently made with him was now lost.

Sighing, she stretched her legs and rested her feet
nearer the fire. What an idiot she was! She shouldn't
have bothered to ask whether Thursday's dinner party
had business motives behind it, she should have known
it had—otherwise it would not be she who was asked to
be hostess.

The frustrating thing was that she hadn't really been reluctant to play this role, because lately there had been moments when she'd actually found herself liking her boss. Her admiration for him as a businessman was enormous, and today she had seen several sides of Leon Silver, the man. His relationship with his grandmother was a good one and it had been very clear that his children both adored and respected him. She had seen also that on his part there was a fine combination of discipline and love.

Was he with them now? Had he gone on to Buckinghamshire to spend the week-end with his family? She looked at her watch; it was not yet nine, and an inexplicable restlessness was taking hold of her. There again, maybe he'd gone on to somewhere in town, had a date with the beautiful blonde? He had to have some relaxation in life.

'Oh, Cherry!' She laughed scornfully at herself for beating about the bush. What she really wondered was whether he was in fact spending the week-end with the blonde, in the penthouse, since his children were out of the way . . .

An hour later she got into bed, having toyed with the idea of taking a walk and having decided against it. By midnight she realised she should have, she should have taken a very long walk because there was no way she could sleep. And it was too late to go out alone now. She was thinking about the incident in the lift and her reaction to it. Maybe it was just as well that Leon was being cool with her. Cool? Cold. As cold as he'd been in the early days.

But maybe it *was* just as well.

She turned over and thumped her pillow into a more comfy position, trying very hard to convince herself of this. And yet . . . and yet she couldn't. Not quite. There was a great deal of confusion inside her. On the one hand she was fascinated by him, frustrated by the unpleasant way this evening had ended, his curt

'Goodnight' and no more. On the other hand, she didn't really like the man. Well, not much, not wholly. And the realisation that she was physically attracted to him appalled her because she didn't want to feel that way towards any man.

# CHAPTER SIX

CHERRY stood back from the dining table and eyed it critically. She gave a satisfied nod, fiddled for just a moment with the flowers which were the centrepiece and then went into the guest room to change.

She wasn't in the least nervous about the dinner party but she was unhappy, generally unhappy. It was Thursday, and, since she had tomorrow off, this was her last working day before the Christmas holiday. The past four days had been busy and they should have been fun because much of her time had been taken up by luncheons, the office party which had gone on for hours and, this morning, yet another 'Christmas drink' which had been held in the board room for fifth floor staff. There had been very little work going on in the building for the last couple of days—which was only to be expected at this time of year.

Leon Silver's attitude was the cause of her unhappiness. They had reverted to the minimum of communication between them, talking only when necessary and never about anything other than work or whatever function they'd been attending. Twice when she'd been off the premises with him he had given her a lift home, again with a curt farewell and no other comments.

Cherry found this frustrating, upsetting, but she had accepted it and had quelled her inclination to try and change things, to get back on to that footing which had been acquired over the past few weeks. Heaven knew that it had been delicate to start with, and now it had gone. Oh, he wasn't being unpleasant, exactly. He was just—cold. There wasn't even any sarcasm, no goading her into a response, there was just this cold neutrality which was worse than anything. In fact most of the time he seemed vaguely preoccupied, as though there was a worry on his mind which took his attention even while he was working or in the middle of a conversation with someone. It didn't detract from his efficiency, and someone less sensitive than Cherry might not even notice it, but she knew it was there. He resented her, she had thought this from the very start. She was convinced of it now.

Alec Moore would be back at the end of January. Thank goodness for that. He was back in England, had telephoned the office several times, wanting to know what was afoot, talking for ages to the MD. Still, there was another month to go, weeks during which she would be working with Leon—and she wished things could be different between them.

She put the finishing touches to her make-up, dabbed perfume behind her ears and took a long look at herself in the mirror. The cream-coloured cashmere dress she was wearing hugged her slender curves and showed them off to their best advantage. It had a scoop neck, long sleeves, and with the gold leather belt at the waist it was sufficiently dressy without overdoing things. She stepped into her shoes and brushed her hair vigorously before putting on her plain gold necklace and earrings.

Idiot. Again she told herself she was pathetic because last Saturday she had gone out and spent a fortune on this dress—and she'd chosen it with Leon Silver's preference in mind. It was not black. She smiled, pleased with her reflection. It was worth every penny!

Closing the lid on the electric curlers she'd carried to work that morning, she put them in her vanity case. Her hair was too long, too heavy to curl without a little assistance and she was wearing it down tonight. It looked good, a shiny cascade of very dark brown hair which reached beyond her shoulders. Would Leon like it loose like this?

Would Leon even notice?

A knock on the door shattered her train of thought. The catering manageress popped her head into the room, an apologetic expression on her face. 'Sorry to interrupt you, Mrs Simson. Everything's ready. Are you sure you wouldn't like me to stay and serve dinner?'

Cherry smiled. Mrs Morrison was priceless. 'Thanks, but no. I think you've done more than enough already. I won't see you tomorrow so I'll wish you a happy Christmas now.'

'And a happy Christmas to you, Mrs Simson! Good-night then.'

Anne Mellor had long since decided what would be served tonight; Mrs Morrison had personally done the cooking, so all that remained for Cherry to do was take the food from the kitchen to the dining table. And she wouldn't even have had to do that had Graham O'Connell not been on holiday. He'd gone to Ireland for a couple of weeks, to spend Christmas and New Year with friends.

Cherry went into the kitchen to check on things a few minutes later. There was so little for her to do, actually! She'd have been perfectly at home doing the cooking herself, that was one task which never daunted her because she loved it.

The slamming of a door made her turn swiftly, looking expectantly in the direction of the hall. Was that Mrs Morrison leaving or was it Leon emerging from his bedroom?

'Mrs Simson?' The deep voice came from the living room and she walked smartly towards it.

'I'm here. Is everything——' She broke off, waiting for some comment as his eyes flicked rapidly over her and then began a slow, detailed surveillance. 'Well?'

'Well what?'

She sighed. Aloud. If he wanted her to spell it out, she would. 'Well, do you approve?'

'Does it matter to you?'

'I think we've had this conversation before. Yes, Mr Silver, it matters.'

He smiled slightly but his voice was as cold as ever. 'Then yes, I approve very much. Especially the hair.' He went over to the drinks cabinet, turning to her. 'What would you like to drink?'

'Something strong.'

'Is anything wrong?'

'No. Yes.' She bit her lip. Everything was wrong, everything! Him, this awful tension between them, this unspoken—whatever it was! 'Mr Silver, I can't help wondering——'

'Do you think,' he cut in, 'that you could possibly bring yourself to call me Leon, at least when we're not in the office? Or would that be too much of an imposition? Granted, you are on duty tonight but . . .' He shrugged as he handed her a glass, obviously satisfied that he'd made his point.

Cherry's eyes closed briefly. She was pleased yet irritated at the same time. 'Yes, I think I can manage that. I could even go as far as enjoying myself tonight if you'd stop being so damned hostile!'

'Hostile? *You're* accusing *me*——' The buzzing of the internal telephone stopped him and he threw her an impatient look. 'Our guests have arrived. Is everything ready?'

'Of course.' She sat down while he answered the phone, hearing his brief conversation with the night watchman before he went down to meet his guests. In the few moments she had alone she sipped at the drink he'd given her, pulling a face and abandoning the glass as she realised it was neat whisky.

What a classic, his thinking *she* was being hostile! She picked up the drink again, thoughtful. Was she? Could it be that her constant awareness of him was making her transmit hostile vibes? As a sort of . . . a sort of counter-action.

Counter-action against what? Leon showed no sign

whatever of finding her physically attractive. Even the kiss they'd shared had left him about as impressed as an Eskimo might be with a snowfall!

Oh, Lord, *why* did she keep analysing, why was he constantly on her mind, in or out of the office?

It was a relief when the evening got under way, and it all went very smoothly indeed. At least as far as the guests were concerned. Dinner was a masterpiece and Cherry made it clear that no credit was due to her. The only awkward moment was towards the end of the evening, when they were all relaxing in the living room, by which time the guests had had a fair amount to drink.

The oldest man present was the MD of an engineering company with whom Silver & Silver did mutual business. He was also the one who'd consumed the most wine with the meal, the most brandy after his coffee. 'Enchanting, Leon!' he said suddenly and quite out of context, in a moment when his eyes came to rest on Cherry. 'I've been meaning to congratulate you all evening on finding such a beautiful secretary. What a pity she's spoken for, eh? I can see that you two have more in common than the welfare of Silver & Silver! Am I right, Leon?'

Leon merely smiled. He caught Cherry's eyes in his cold green gaze and put the ball in her court. 'What would you say, Cherry?'

She said very little. She treated the older man to her most charming smile, her slender hands moving in an attitude which told him she had nothing to declare—nothing at all. 'Being interested in Silver & Silver is all we need in common. That makes for a successful business relationship.'

'But doesn't your husband object? I mean, your working after hours like this?' The question came from the woman Leon had referred to as a 'mistress'.

'I can hardly call this work,' Cherry said lightly. She was not going to volunteer her marital status—it would only leave things open for more speculation from the elderly man who'd started all this. He had successfully trained everyone's eyes on her and for the first time that evening, she felt uncomfortable. Hitherto she'd been too busy playing hostess to worry about anything, including her boss, though she was incapable of relaxing completely in his presence.

She didn't get away with it though. The next question was specific and couldn't be dodged. It was the mistress again. 'But surely he can't like it! I mean, you're so young. How long have you been married, actually?'

'Cherry is a widow.' It came from Leon. He spoke with a subtle edge to his voice which told everyone that this conversation should stop there.

It worked. Everyone was surprised, the mistress apologetic. The man who'd had too much to drink, however, made one final comment. 'Ah! There's another thing you have in common.'

The evening continued, the conversation becoming more jovial and light as time passed. The guests departed at a little after one, having enjoyed themselves, and taking care to say so.

Cherry bade them goodbye at the door to the penthouse, leaving Leon to see them off the premises. By the time he came back she'd cleared the dining table and stacked everything in the dishwasher.

'Cherry...'

He was standing about two feet behind her but the noise of the machine had covered the sound of his footsteps. She jumped, turning to face him. 'Oh, I—I didn't hear you come back.'

He didn't say anything. He looked at her for several seconds and she hadn't the faintest idea what was going through his mind. All she could be sure of was that a wall was descending between them again, and it made her terribly sad.

'... I'll run you home now.'

She nodded. What was the use? Hadn't she said herself that all she and he needed was a successful business relationship? Well, they had that, just about. The work got done.

She picked up her bag, fetched her vanity case and her stole, and grew more and more tense as she travelled down in the lift with him. Would she ever ride in a lift—any lift—and not think of what had happened the time she'd experienced being trapped in one?

'Wait here,' he said when they reached the main entrance. 'I'll bring the car round.'

He was just pulling up when the night watchman appeared, saying a quick hello and goodbye and he hoped she'd had a nice evening.

Leon opened the car door for her. She slipped into the passenger seat, pulling her stole closely around her shoulders, shivering against the cold night air.

And then there was a silent journey to Hampstead. He pulled up outside her house, and only then was something said, when Cherry could stand it no longer. 'Leon——'

'I want to thank you.' He wasn't looking at her and his voice was level, almost flat. 'You were—it was a very successful evening and I'm grateful to you.'

'Grateful? There's no need——'

'And I'm sorry about old Felix putting you on the spot like that, his vague insinuations. He meant no harm, he'd had too much to drink.'

'I know. Leon——' She took her courage in both hands, willing him to look at her. 'Please come in and have a cup of coffee.'

'Why, Mrs Simson——'

'*Stop it!*' Her violet eyes flashed in the lamplight and she turned her head away. She was in danger of losing her temper, which was almost unheard of for her. 'I want to talk to you, all right? Just say yes or no!'

'Has it anything to do with business?'

Her gasp of irritation was audible over the gentle hum of the engine and she turned to glare at him with eyes which were irresistibly beautiful, had she but known it. And then she was laughing because she saw he was grinning, an audacious, roguish grin. It made all her anger melt away, and she sighed helplessly. 'As a matter of fact, it has.'

'Then I accept.' He inclined his head, his white teeth catching the light as his grin became the most attractive of smiles.

Leon was intrigued. Why the invitation? She had recently taken a step backward in their relationship, was she now taking a step forward? Or did she really want to talk business? He stilled the engine, got out of the car and opened the door for her. 'Your key?' He held out his hand and she dropped her door key into his palm. 'Never let it be said that I have no time for business, mm?'

'Never!'

He shed his dark mood as easily as he had shed his overcoat once they were inside her living room, when he complimented her on her comfortable surroundings.

Cherry started talking, suddenly light-hearted, and it seemed she couldn't stop. Before making coffee she showed him around and they ended up in the kitchen, she explaining how she came to rent the house, how lucky she'd been.

Leon took the coffee tray from her and put it on the low table in front of the settee. Without reference to her he switched off the overhead light and turned on two table lamps which left the room softly lit. He also turned the fire up so the glow of the flames became a dance which added cosiness to the atmosphere. It was only then that she had a momentary qualm about the wisdom of inviting him into her home so late at night.

She needn't have worried. He sat facing her, away from her, filling an armchair, his long legs stretched out in front of the log fire. He looked utterly relaxed, at home, though she could now see a tiredness in his face which she hadn't noticed earlier. He worked too hard, far too hard. He started at seven and he finished at eight or nine. At least, she thought he did. For all she knew, he might work till midnight. It wouldn't have surprised her.

She put his coffee on a side table near his chair. Silence reigned for several minutes while they drank, but there was no awkwardness in it, no tension. How, why this should be, so suddenly, she had no idea. She was just grateful for it.

'How long were you married, in fact?' His question was point blank and it seemed to come after a train of thought.

'My husband was killed while we were on our honeymoon,' she said quietly, her answer coming spontaneously and without any hesitation. 'On our wedding day, to be precise. We'd been married for barely ten hours . . .'

His eyes caught hers and they allowed her to know exactly how the information affected him. 'Christ, I'm so sorry! How awful . . .'

She dipped her head in acknowledgment, leaning back against the cushions of the settee. 'And you?'

'I was married to Andrea for six years, the twins were three when she died,' he spoke normally, unemotionally. 'She was very ill with cancer for a long time, they barely remember her. Your husband—I take it there was an accident?'

'A car crash. We were in France. After the wedding reception we drove down to Portsmouth and took the ferry to Cherbourg. We were in our own car and we were only about thirty kilometres from the hotel we'd booked for the night. We were going to drive on to Paris the following day, spend a week there and then drive on to Italy for the second week. Anyhow, it was dark, it was raining and—I suppose David was tired. The accident was his fault. He took a bend too quickly, too near the centre of the road . . .'

A curious thing happened to her as she talked. For the first time ever she felt detached, uninvolved, as if the people she was talking about were strangers. 'There was a head-on collision and I came out of it with a bruise on the cheek bone and a broken wrist. God knows how! David was killed outright, so was the driver of the other car.'

She talked on, without pain or emotion of any kind, telling Leon the details as she remembered them, patchy though they were. 'I can't decide which is worse,' she said at length, 'I mean, you lost your wife after six years, but you had those six years with her. I had . . . but maybe it's better that way. Maybe it would have been even worse if I'd had——'

'Don't do that, Cherry. Neither you nor I can answer that question, so don't try. Love isn't something you can measure in time or by pouring into a bucket to see how much there is.'

She laughed quietly, soft laughter which brought a smile to her lips, making it impossible for Leon to take his eyes off her. 'How complicated life could get if one could do that!'

His smile was wry. 'But if we could, I'd say that your bucket will be filled to the brim when you discover love all over again. You'll remarry, given time.'

The smile faded from her lips, from her eyes. 'I doubt that very much.'

'I said in time. You'll see.'

'Can you envisage yourself remarrying, Leon?'

'Envisage?' Very firmly he said, 'I have every intention of doing so.' Then he laughed and picked up his cup and saucer and rattled them, laughing even more at the look on her face.

'Dear me!' She looked heavenward. 'Could that possibly mean you're still thirsty, I wonder?'

She poured more coffee and they talked on, and on. It was only when the clock chimed on the hour that she realised how late it was, that she'd virtually told him her life story! And when next the clock chimed, she shut up at once, almost embarrassed at the way she'd chattered on about herself. But he'd prompted her, he'd encouraged her . . . then he'd sat back and done most of the listening. 'Leon, it's four o'clock in the morning!'

'So what? You don't have to get up early tomorrow.'

'No, but you do.'

'My dear Cherry, I don't *have* to do any such thing.'

He was right, of course. Nevertheless he got up quickly, without preamble, and she looked up in surprise. 'I fear I've bored you, Leon! All at once you can't wait to get away!'

He looked at her, every inch of her, deeply disturbed by the picture she made. How unaware she was of her beauty, sitting there like that, her long legs curled under her, the swirl of dark hair when she tossed her head back, laughing, the incredible blue of her eyes . . .

He ought to go. He *had* to go. *Now*. The self-discipline, the self-control which was so much a part of his nature was slipping, had been eroding steadily tonight with every tick of the clock.

He smiled to himself, at himself. The erosion hadn't started tonight, not by any means! He'd wanted this woman for a long time, had looked at her a dozen times a day and wanted to make love to her there and then—anywhere, anytime, all the time . . .

'I wish you'd say something!' Cherry looked up at him, laughing a little uncertainly. 'Your silence is confirming what I said!'

'Is it? Then it just goes to show how wrong you can be.' He bent suddenly to take hold of her hands, pulling her to her feet.

Cherry's stomach tightened, the touch of his hands, his nearness sending shivers along the surface of her skin. Dear God, he was so attractive, so big and broad and powerful! 'What's wrong, Leon?' She felt her mouth go dry, had to moisten her lips before she could go on. 'Why are you looking at me like that?'

It seemed an eternity passed before he answered her. She felt as though she were drowning in the intense green of his eyes, eyes which were looking at her in a way they'd never looked at her before. His voice was gravelly as he spoke, deep and very quiet. 'Cherry, if I stay here any longer I shall make love to you. That's what's wrong.'

It took her breath away. Her eyes widened, her lips parted but no words came out. *Make love* to her? 'I—but I——' She resorted to flippancy; it was the only way she could cover her floundering, her astonishment. 'You made that sound as though I'd have no say in the matter!'

He just smiled, drawing her against him and kissing her before she had any chance of escape. But this time she didn't want to escape. And this time he kissed her differently. It began with a savagery she welcomed because she'd waited so long to know once again the feel of his lips on hers. She hadn't realised that until now, she hadn't realised she was not merely attracted to this man, she was hungry for him!

Sweet sensations exploded within her as his kiss changed from a raw and blatant demand to a subtle coaxing which turned her hunger into an aching need. Leon's arousal was obvious, immediate, but he was in control and it was he who set the pace, kissing her differently all the time she was locked in his arms—teasing, withdrawing, exploring until finally she wrenched away from him, gasping and shocked by an expertise she had never before encountered, an excitement that made her head spin.

Not a word was spoken as they looked at each other, standing two feet apart. Then Leon's eyes moved to the soft curves of her breasts, their rise and fall as she fought to control her breathing, and the slight move he made drew a frightened protest from her. She stepped swiftly away from him. 'No, Leon!' If he touched her body she'd be lost, completely lost.

As it was she had some control, enough to realise what a ghastly mistake she'd made, what he must be thinking of her now! 'Leon, please! I—I didn't invite you in to ... for ...'

'I'm aware of that.' His eyes closed briefly and he let out a long, slow breath. 'Unfortunately, I'm very well aware of it.'

She turned away from him, feeling guilty for some unfathomable reason. 'I—all I wanted tonight was to get to know you better, to improve our relationship.'

His low laughter brought her swiftly round to face him as she realised what she'd said. 'I didn't—you know what I meant, Leon! Right from the start there was animosity between us, and this last week has been unbearable, the tension has been so upsetting and—and all I wanted to do was to put an end to it.' She looked away, feeling silly. She couldn't blame him for getting the wrong impression. But if she'd known he was attracted to her, she'd never have invited——

'Cherry ... Cherry, come here.'

'No! I've told you, I——'

'All right, all right. You don't need to draw pictures for me. But look at me, at least, because it seems that the same can't be said for you.'

She looked at him. 'What do you mean?'

'I mean that for a twenty-four-year-old woman who went as far as the altar with the last man in her life, you're incredibly naive. There is not, there never has been, any animosity between us. It exists only in your mind—and animosity is quite the wrong word. What you're really referring to is the physical attraction we both felt from the start. As for your other expression ... the tension you refer to is real enough.' He smiled humourlessly, the deadly serious eyes denying her the ability to look away. 'I don't think I need to say more, you know what the remedy is.'

Cherry's heart was pounding with alarm. She was hearing the truth and it was unwelcome. 'You—you don't mince your words, do you? You've certainly got to the heart of the matter!' Her attempt at laughter came out hollowly, leaving him unmoved. His face was impassive and he might just as well have been talking about tomorrow's weather forecast.

'Since when did I call a spade a digging implement? Cherry, listen to me and remember what I'm telling you. David is dead. You are alive and young and a very desirable woman. You are also desirous. You want me as much as I want you—but there's a difference. I have no justifications to make. Neither do you, in fact, but you think you have. It's only a matter of time before we become lovers. You need time, and I'll give it to you. But believe me, when *I* decide that the time is right to make love to you, you *won't* have any say in the matter.'

He picked up his overcoat and made for the door. 'Goodnight, Cherry. Take care of yourself and have a good Christmas. I'll see myself out.'

He left, closing the front door quietly behind him. As he started the engine of the Rolls, he glanced at the house. He put his arms on the steering wheel and stared out into the wet blackness of the street, frowning. From the very beginning he'd known some things about her almost instinctively, and he'd learned more with every passing week.

But there was something about her, somehow, which didn't quite add up, and he was damned if he could figure it out . . .

# CHAPTER SEVEN

'WHAT's wrong, Cherry? I can't decide whether you're sickening for something or just plain bored!'

Bored? No, it wasn't that, not quite. It was just that she didn't want to be at home, that the Christmas holiday was too long. She was missing Leon so much it was almost painful. There was a long time to go before she'd see him again, before she could get back to work, to normal.

She was standing by the window in her parents' living room, motionless, looking out. Frost lay thickly on the grass, the trees in the garden were bare and starkly outlined against a sky which was white with clouds. Outside there was that peculiar stillness of a Boxing Day morning, no sound of traffic, giving the impression it was far earlier than ten o'clock, that the day had not yet begun.

Inside the house there was a certain lethargy which had enveloped not only Cherry but her mother and her sister-in-law. The males of the family had gone for a walk, Cherry's four-year-old nephew included. Behind her there was the persistent click-click of her mother's knitting needles, the sound of magazine pages being turned over by Julie. 'Nothing's wrong, Mum. I was just . . . thinking.'

'Thinking?' Her mother looked up, frowning. 'You've been preoccupied for days! What's bothering you? Is it your job?'

'No, I——'

'Is it your boss?' This question came from Julie and she was giving Cherry a searching look. 'Dad says he's a very attractive man. You haven't fallen for him, have you?'

'Don't be ridiculous!'

'Hey, there's no need to bite my head off! I only——'

'I'm sorry, Julie. I——' She looked at her sister-in-law apologetically, seeing the hurt expression on her face. Julie was a pretty girl, normally slim and petite, but barrel-like now with her second pregnancy. 'No, I haven't fallen for him.' She turned back to the window, hoping she'd just told the truth.

'Of course you haven't!' Her mother didn't even consider it a possibility. Her mother had never met Leon Silver. 'But you're getting on with him much better these days, aren't you?'

'Yes, Mum. I'm—getting on with him very well. Look, I think I'll go out for a walk, it'll give me an appetite for lunch. Maybe I'll catch up with the men . . .'

She left the house five minutes later, her sheepskin coat buttoned up to the neck. She had no intention of catching up with the men, she wanted to be alone, to think.

To think? She'd done nothing but think since that night with Leon! His face floated constantly before her eyes, his name was forever on her lips. How positively, certainly, he'd told her they were going to be lovers! Was he right? How could he *know* with such certainty? And why did the prospect fill her as much with trepidation as it did with excitement?

With her head down, her hands shoved deep inside her pockets, she walked slowly in the direction of the park. Of course he was right. If he made up his mind to make love to her, she wouldn't be able to resist him. *That's* what he knew.

And that wasn't all. He'd said she needed time, why had he said that? Why should he think that, when she was by no means recently widowed? Above all, how come he was right in what he'd said? She did need time. If she were contemplating an affair with him, she should at least know how she felt about the man . . .

And she was contemplating it.

But she didn't know how she felt about him.

All she was sure of at this instant was that she missed him acutely. The days, Christmas or otherwise, were dull and flat without him and she couldn't wait to see him again.

'Cherry? Cherry!'

She looked up. She had walked into the park, idiot that she was. It was the obvious place for her father and brother to have taken Christopher. Resignedly she waved and hurried over to them, scooping her nephew into her arms as he started his own delightful brand of chatter.

It snowed that night, and the next day found her in the garden with the four-year old, building a snowman.

New Year's Eve found her in bed with a stinking cold. There was a party going on downstairs and she felt utterly miserable, frustrated, aching and blue. She should return to work the day after tomorrow, and she *had* to be better by then! What a stupid thing to do, catching a cold! She'd spent too much time in the freezing outdoors and she felt as though the marrow of her bones had frozen solid.

'Cherry? Are you awake?' It was Julie who brought her a cup of tea the next morning. 'Happy New Year! Mmm—well, you know what I mean! I must say you look awful!'

'Thanks, pal.' She struggled to a sitting position, groaning at the effort. 'Julie, you shouldn't be in here. I think it's 'flu. Oh, I'm aching all over!'

'Oh, crumbs! Then Christopher's probably in for it, poor little thing. He woke up with the sniffles this morning.'

'Happy New Year to you, too, Julie . . .'

'Hello, Penny. It's Cherry. Is Mr Silver in?' Her hand tightened on the telephone receiver, the anticipation of talking to Leon almost more than she could stand.

She had been in bed at her parents' home for a whole week and her father had phoned the office for her, to explain her absence. He'd spoken with the boss himself, fortunately, and had been able to pass on to Cherry the get well soon message which had pleased her to a ridiculous extent.

Only yesterday had she driven back to London, and, from the way she was feeling, it had been a day too soon. She was still tired, and while she'd had every intention of going into work this morning, common sense had made her stay at home for one more day. Tomorrow. She would see him tomorrow and then she would feel whole again.

'Happy New Year, Cherry! Bit late, but still. How are you? Are you better? We thought you'd be in this morning . . .' Penny chattered on, obviously unharried. 'Mr Silver is in but he's got the people from Cooper's Beers Head Office with him. They came first thing and they'll probably be talking for hours.'

'Oh.' Her heart sank. 'What . . .? Good grief, no, don't disturb him! Just—just tell him I'll be in in the morning. Are you coping all right?'

Poor Penny, she started to defend herself immediately, explaining that she wouldn't have suggested disturbing Mr Silver for anyone else and that she was coping very well. Really and truly! 'But I'm not sure what's going to happen around here. Anne handed her notice in last week and——'

'Her *notice*? What—why? Is she ill?'

'No. Well, I don't think so. You know she never tells you much. I think—oh, the other line's ringing, I'd better go. See you tomorrow, Cherry.'

They hung up. Cherry made herself a pot of tea and put her feet up on the sofa. Anne had handed her notice in? So what happened now?

She slept most of the afternoon away, got up and watched televison until midnight and then slept like a log until morning. She wasn't feeling on top of the world physically the next day but she was well enough to go back to work. Besides, she couldn't wait any longer . . .

It was something of an effort but she got to work at nine and went straight to the ladies' room to check on her appearance, her stomach filled with a hundred butterflies. She had recognised the symptoms days ago. She ought to, she'd been in love once before. But she'd told herself over and over that she was mistaken, that she felt only physical attraction for Leon Silver, nothing more permanent . . . more potentially damaging.

And it was that which had made her play the stupid game of denying it, denying it to herself as well as to others. More potentially damaging. She was afraid. Afraid of loving again, afraid of losing again. For what was it he felt for her? Desire, certainly. But was there anything else on his part?

If there were, she saw no sign of it in his eyes when she walked into his office ten minutes later. Anne was with him, her notebook and pencil on her lap, and they both wished Cherry a happy new year, said they were glad to see her back.

It was such an anti-climax. Her disappointment on finding Anne in his office was enormous and she told herself off for being ridiculous again. He was wearing the suit she liked best, navy blue with a fine pin-stripe, and a crisp white shirt which was unbuttoned at the neck so the black hair on his chest was just visible. He was always like this when there were no visitors around, his tie loosened, his shirt undone at the collar, no jacket, just his waistcoat . . .

She wanted to feast her eyes on him, to drink in the details of his face and his thick, dark hair until she'd made up for two weeks of not seeing him. As it was, she gave him a smile and a polite greeting, sitting down when he invited her to do so.

'Well,' he began, 'which would you like first, Cherry, the bad news or the good?'

Cherry looked at Anne, knowing what the bad news was. She couldn't say so, however, that wouldn't be fair to Penny. 'Why not tell me in that order?'

'Anne is leaving us on Friday.'

'On *Friday*?' Her surprise was not feigned; she hadn't expected Anne's notice to be so short! 'Is something wrong, Anne, are you ill?'

'My blood pressure's too high and I can't say I'm feeling tip-top.' She shrugged, looking as smart as a new pin despite her pregnant state. She really wasn't very big, considering, not compared to Julie. 'I wanted to stay on till the last minute, as you know.' She looked from Cherry to Leon, obviously none too happy. 'But my husband's put his foot down and—well, frankly, I'm simply not up to it.'

Leon smiled but said nothing. The silence encouraged Anne to go on, and Cherry was surprised at the way she opened up. 'It's odd, really. I want this baby desperately and I'm looking forward so much to a new lifestyle, a very different lifestyle from the one I've had during the past fourteen years. I've been married ten years, Cherry, and we've been hoping for a baby all that time. And yet . . .' she broke off, her laughter soft and self-deprecating. 'I'm also a bit scared to let go of my old lifestyle. I'm thirty-nine years old and I'm pregnant with my first child. It's due in fourteen weeks—and I'll be forty by then!'

Feeling curiously grateful to her for her openness, Cherry smiled warmly. She'd known all along that Anne's relationship with her boss was pretty special— and how nice that she too was now privy to a side of Anne's personality she'd never seen before. Hitherto she'd never spoken about herself, never gossiped, never tried to make friends with Cherry. Indeed she'd always held herself deliberately aloof. 'If it's any consolation, let me tell you that my mother was forty when she had me. Granted, I was her second child, but still.'

'There you are!' Leon put in. 'And look at Cherry. She's turned out okay.' He smiled, the green gaze sweeping over the younger woman, sending a delicious tremor through her. 'Well, more or less!'

'Thank you very much, Mr Silver! Now what's the good news?'

He got back to business, and straight to the point, as usual. 'Yesterday, the personnel manager had a visit from Karen Black. Did you meet her? The girl who used to work for Alec? She was with us for six years and she was extremely good at her job. Alec thought the world of her.'

'But—but she was going back to New Zealand to get married! Why is she back in England?'

Leon shrugged. 'I don't know. I don't even know whether she got as far as New Zealand. All I know is that she's in London, that she called in to say she was available and if there were any suitable vacancies in the company, she wanted to be considered. Now, I spoke to Alec on the phone yesterday—he's coming back next week, by the way . . .'

Cherry looked down at the carpet. She could see what was coming and she didn't want to show her delight, didn't want him to know that she could refuse him nothing. He was about to ask her if she would work as his secretary permanently, and she would say yes. Yes, yes, yes!

But he didn't ask her. He told her. 'Alec agreed with me that in view of all the circumstances, you should work with me, Cherry. Since you have some experience with my work, and Karen knows Alec's work inside out, we reached the obvious conclusion.'

'I see.'

'You've no objection, I take it.'

She didn't quite meet his eyes, didn't want him to know how happy this made her. As casually as possible, she said no, she had no objections.

'Good.' He was so businesslike now, presenting her

with a *fait accompli*—to which there was more. 'Anne's made all the travel arrangements for Nairobi. We're flying out on Sunday. We'll be there the whole of next week.'

Cherry fiddled with the rings on her finger, looking away again. She hadn't expected this! She was pleased by the prospect of a trip to Kenya but it came as a shock to her. His visit to Nairobi must have been discussed with Cooper's yesterday. She'd known he would have to go out there, that he'd have to liaise with the architects who were working on the plans for the new brewery just outside Nairobi. Alec's part with Cooper's business was finished, it was Leon's baby now.

'Is something wrong, Cherry?' There was a tinge of amusement in his voice, though his face was impassive.

'No, I——' There was and there wasn't. It was going to be very different indeed, wasn't it, working with him abroad? They'd be together during the evenings, every evening, probably . . . Did he *really* need her to go with him or did he have some ulterior motive for taking her away? Would this be the start of an affair she was by no means sure she wanted, by no means sure she could handle? Anne got up then. 'I'll press on, Mr Silver, if there's nothing else?'

'All right, Anne. It might be an idea for you and Cherry to get together over lunch or something. You can brief her about Nairobi.'

'I was going to suggest that myself.' Anne looked questioningly at Cherry. 'Lunch—today? We'll go out, I think, that way there'll be no interruptions.'

'That's fine with me.' They fixed a time and Anne left the office just as the telephone rang.

Leon picked it up, 'No, don't go, Cherry. I'd like a word . . . Hello, Penny. Who? Ah, yes, put them through . . .'

For several minutes Cherry sat in a state of nervous anxiety which was mingled with anticipation. She would have to go shopping on Saturday. She was short on summer clothes, and it would be hot in Africa . . . She'd have to ring her parents and tell them she'd be away for a week. A week with Leon . . .

The minutes ticked away while he talked, seeming like hours. She wanted to know what he'd say to her when he finished his call, how he'd look at her, what his attitude would be. Then she glanced at him only to find that his eyes were on her, and they were telling her nothing at all.

He dropped the receiver on to its cradle. 'How are you feeling, Cherry?'

'Oh, about eighty percent,' she smiled.

'I wasn't referring to your physical condition, though I'm sorry you're not up to scratch. Don't overdo it today. Go home early if you want to.' He put an elbow on his desk, resting his head against a fist. 'You looked positively scared when I mentioned our trip next week. Why?'

'I—it just came as a surprise, that's all. You'd never mentioned you'd be taking me with you.'

'Surely you didn't think I'd be taking Anne, in her condition?'

'Hardly!'

'And so?' When she didn't answer, he smiled a knowing smile.

So he knew full well what her reservations were! She looked away, hating herself for the blush which was rising from the base of her throat.

Leon opened his desk drawer and pulled out a long, flat envelope. 'My children are upstairs. I have to take them back to school later. Term starts in the morning. Last week they asked me to give this to my . . . "dogsbody". *Dogsbody*, Cherry?'

She groaned, his tone of voice serving nicely to deepen the blush on her face. 'That was just a— something I said on the spur of the moment. A joke.'

'The twins got a good telling off.'

'Oh, no! But it was entirely my fault, they didn't know the meaning of the word!'

'So I discovered—after I'd told them off.'

Cherry felt awful. 'I'm going upstairs to see them, I must apologise!' She knew what it was like to be on the receiving end of a telling off from Leon Silver. She took the envelope from him, feeling even more guilty, and very touched, when she saw its contents. It was a calendar— a calendar made by eight-year olds, a collage of pictures cut from magazines.

'They tell me it's for your office,' Leon smiled. 'If you can put up with it.'

'Put up with it? It's lovely—er—well, it was a very sweet thought and I'll certainly hang it in my office!' She could just imagine how hurt they'd be if it weren't on show next time they called in. Things like that were very important to children. 'Do you mind, Leon, if I go up to see them?'

'Of course not. O'Connell's with them. Use the stairs then you won't need the lift key.'

Leon's luxuriously furnished living room was being used for a game of hunt-the-thimble, she discovered when she got upstairs. She was instantly forgiven for the telling off she'd caused the twins and was invited to join in their game. She declined, encouraging them to tell her instead about the Christmas presents they'd been given.

Half an hour later she was playing Space Invaders and was thinking, reluctantly, that she really must go and do some work. She was expecting the phone to ring any minute, expecting to hear Leon's voice ordering her downstairs. But the phone didn't ring, he came in person, not to tell her there was work waiting but to ask her if she'd like a drive into the country during the afternoon, when he took the twins back to school. She accepted mainly because the twins urged her to go with them, and partly because she wasn't up to much work that day. Leon realised it, too, which was sweet of him.

Her lunch with Anne lasted over an hour and was largely a waste of time. It was as if Anne now, and only now, considered Cherry to be her equal—which the younger girl found vaguely amusing. After fourteen years with Leon she was handing over to someone else, and she obviously thought that anyone good enough to be the new secretary to the Chairman and MD of Silver & Silver deserved to be given as much information as possible about him. After talking about the arrangements for the trip to Nairobi, and pointing out that Leon always travelled first class, 'naturally', it was this information Anne moved on to next.

But it all came too late. All the pointers she gave about Leon's character and his methods of working were things that Cherry had already learned first hand. It would have been more helpful of Anne to have talked openly about her boss several months ago.

Cherry did learn one thing, however, and it was this alone which made her lunch date with Anne worthwhile, very worthwhile. It was something which had nothing to do with the point of their lunching together and they were just leaving the restaurant when Anne came out with it.

'Oh, sugar!' She turned to Cherry, looking appalled. 'You see, I'm just *not* myself at the moment! I forgot to pass on Mrs Reynold's message to Mr Silver before I left the building! He wasn't around when she rang. I hope she's still at home ... she said she's leaving for Paris this afternoon and she wanted him to ring her back before two-thirty!'

'Mrs Reynolds?'

'His lady friend, Heidi Reynolds.'

Cherry slipped into her coat, avoiding Anne's eyes. 'Oh, yes, I believe I spoke to her once.' She knew full well she'd spoken to the woman, the woman who'd described herself as a 'friend' of Mr Silver. 'Er—in fact, I think I've seen her. Is she blonde, by any chance? And very tall? Have you met her?'

'That's right. Yes, I've met her several times. She rarely calls into the office but I've arranged dinner parties in the penthouse, and met her then. She always insists on choosing the menu herself if she's playing hostess.'

'Oh, I—got the impression that Mr Silver keeps business separate from pleasure. I thought you'd acted as hostess when he's been entertaining business people.'

'I have. I'm talking about social things—nothing to do with business. Friends of theirs.'

Friends of theirs. The words made Leon and Heidi Reynolds sound like a couple in the accepted sense! 'She's a widow, is she, Mrs Reynolds?'

'Divorced. Twice. She told me herself. She's Swiss but both her husbands were—are, I should say, English.'

Cherry managed a smile, making this as girl-to-girl as she could. 'Has Mr Silver been seeing her long?'

'About a year, I think,' Anne didn't seem sure. 'But I don't think he sees her often. He asks me occasionally to book theatre tickets or a table in a restaurant—and I assume it's she who goes with him. There again,' she laughed, 'it could be one or two others I can think of! Actually, Mrs Reynolds is a business woman herself, she has a chain of boutiques and she's very business-orientated. In a way, I suppose she's just right for him, not that that's any of my business.'

Cherry couldn't help herself. Maybe she was going too far, but she had to ask. She felt slightly sick. 'You make it sound as though the relationship is serious, Anne.'

'Serious? I wouldn't know. Mr Silver doesn't tell me everything, obviously! He's very deep, you know. I've travelled with him, worked with him for fourteen years and I know him well, but there's a lot I don't know, too. I sometimes wonder if there's anyone who knows him inside out.'

Cherry absorbed this information and thought about

it. To have asked more questions of Anne would have revealed an interest which went beyond the call of duty, and she hadn't dared. Besides, Anne didn't know about the frequency of Leon's dates with the Reynolds woman; she'd probably told as much as she knew ... which left Cherry with a dozen questions unanswered.

It also left her feeling very, very, angry. So the statuesque blonde and Heidi Reynolds were one and the same person, and Leon had been seeing her for a year! A year! Their relationship may or may not be serious but it sure as anything wasn't a platonic one! Cherry wasn't *that* naive! So what the devil did he mean by telling her—almost warning her—that she and he would be lovers?

That's what *he* thought!

A little thought enabled her to answer her own questions. She didn't go back to her office. Leon wanted to leave for Hertfordshire at four, so she killed an hour in the staff restroom on the third floor because she didn't want to face him until she'd cooled off.

What kind of fool was she that she'd hoped ... well, that she'd hoped he might feel more than physical desire for her? Anne had implied that she knew, or had known of, other women in her boss's life. So it was obvious what this was all about! He played the field, he had Cherry *standing in line* as his next mistress!

*Like hell!*

What a nerve! He hadn't got rid of the old and he was already contemplating the new. Or did he have her in mind as one of a stable?

'You bastard!' She said it over and over in the privacy of the restroom in which she paced about, feeling as angry with herself as she did with him. 'You're a fool, Cherry Simson, a *fool*.'

Her falling in love again had been an impossibility,

but it had happened. And what had she fallen in love with? A two-timer.

'All right, Leon,' she vowed, '*I'll* give *you* time, and when the crunch comes, we'll see who has a say in the matter!'

# CHAPTER EIGHT

HE watched her as she slept, quite fascinated by the long black lashes which fringed her eyes. How beautiful those eyes were when open, how beautiful she looked while asleep.

She was driving him slowly out of his mind.

Her head was resting against his arm, and he kept still, for if he woke her she would draw away from him as she had been drawing away from him for days.

Leon Silver checked his watch, his eyes moving to the window of the plane. Soon they would be landing at Nairobi airport and the aircraft would descend against the background of a sky flooded with the fiery glow of the setting sun. Cherry had slept through the last two hours of the journey while he ... he had spent his time thinking about her. On his lap there was an open journal he hadn't read a word of. All his attention was focused on the woman beside him.

In her shadow-dance of evasion she had moved again, one step forward and one step back. Two steps back. What was she afraid of? Was she afraid, in fact? Or was he reading into this relationship more than was there, simply because he wanted it to be there? No, no that wasn't the case. Self-deception was not one of his failings.

She'd been so light-hearted the other day, laughing and chatting with him and the children all the way to Hertfordshire. But the drive back to London had been very different. Without the presence of the twins she'd had nothing to say to him. This, when he'd expected so much more, when he'd waited two weeks to see her again, over Christmas and while she'd been ill with the 'flu. This, and her point blank refusal to have dinner with him.

But the next day it had been a different story again! Wednesday had given birth to a new girl, serene, more calmly efficient than she'd ever been—and delighted to accept his invitation to dinner that evening.

He shook his head, laughing quietly to himself. His eyes moved down the length of her body and back again, coming to rest on her mouth. Fortunately for her, he could exercise enormous patience over matters which were important to him. And this was important. And how. Female games of cat and mouse were nothing new to him, not by any means. He would allow her a certain amount of fun, so much room in which to play. So much, and no more.

Not one inch more.

'Cherry? Wake up! Wake up, this sunset will be worth seeing. Besides, we'll be landing in twenty minutes and you've got to get yourself together.'

Cherry heard the words and registered the gruff tone of his voice. What the devil was wrong with him now? Was he annoyed because she'd been sleeping instead of going over that boring report from Cooper's Beers? She'd read it twice already.

Blinking, she surfaced from sleep and snapped fully awake when she realised she'd been resting her head against him. Bother! Now what would he read into that? She pulled away from him quickly, straightening her clothes.

Everything had gone beautifully so far, everything according to plan. She'd managed admirably to be her usual self all week and he had not the slightest idea that she was in love with him. Nor would he ever! She'd refused his invitation to dinner the day she'd learned the truth about his relationship with Heidi Reynolds. She'd been too angry to accept. But the following day, she'd dined with him because to have refused again would have been an unnatural thing to do. He'd wanted to talk to her about their business in Nairobi. She had *not*, however, invited him in for coffee when he'd taken her home. Nor had he invited himself in . . . which had surprised her.

That was the trouble. He hadn't laid a finger on her. There was nothing with which she could accuse him, no way she could broach the subject of his personal life even in the most casual way. He hadn't given her an opening, and she was totally puzzled by him. Deep, he certainly was. And even more mysterious! Maybe he'd changed his mind about her, decided he didn't want her after all? Maybe he had enough to cope with, with Heidi Reynolds and an unknown number of others!

'I'll go and freshen up, Leon.' She smiled at him, wondering how she could feel two such differing emotions at the same time. How could she love him and feel resentment, too? Or did she resent him because she loved him? How could she love him at all?

How could she not?

There was a car and driver waiting for them at the airport and they were driven to a hotel on the other side of Nairobi, Cherry spending all the time looking out of the window, fascinated by her first glimpse of Africa. Colour! There seemed to be so much *colour* here, from the gaily colourful clothing of the local people, their very black faces and very white smiles, to the beauty of a sky which was lit dramatically by a sinking sun shooting waves of vivid pinks and reds into its deep and darkening blue.

The low, white-painted building of their hotel was almost obscured from a distance by its surrounding trees and bushes which were ablaze with colour, myriad shades of green, gold, orange, violet. They approached down a driveway which was flanked by rose gardens and outside the main entrance were enormous ceramic pots overflowing with scarlet bougainvillaea.

From the balcony of her room overlooking the rear of the hotel, the view was breathtakingly beautiful. In the distance was the hazy shape of the Ngong Hills, immediately below her the tropical gardens which promised such delights on closer inspection. She stood, enjoying the perfume of clear, sun-drenched air and flowers and plants, enjoying the stillness, the silence which was disturbed only by the solitary occupant of a glistening blue swimming pool which was surrounded by palm trees.

Excitement rushed through her, an appreciation of the loveliness of everything around her, from her room to all that she could see out here, an appreciation of how very good it was to be alive!

Leon's knock on her bedroom door served only to intensify that excitement, and she turned, calling that the door was open, to come in.

'Everything all right, Cherry? Is there anything you need?' He had already bathed and changed his clothes. His hair was still damp, curling behind his ears where it almost touched the collar of his shirt. He was wearing blue slacks and a lightweight jacket which was snow white.

She smiled, her heart skipping a beat and then racing as she looked at him, loving him, filled with a yearning to touch him, to run her fingers through the thickness of his hair, to feel his arms around her. She looked away as he walked towards her, her hands going nervously to the railing of the balcony. She would have to be on guard, very much so . . . 'Everything's perfect, Leon.'

He stood beside her, making appreciative comments about the view, the sunset, and Cherry edged away from him slightly, disturbed by his nearness, the tang of his aftershave, the sheer size of him as he moved towards her, his hands covering hers. 'Relax, why don't you?' He loosened her fingers from their grip on the railing.

She looked at him uncertainly, hoping her eyes didn't show the alarm she was feeling, her hands dropping to her sides.

He smiled slowly, the green gaze taking in every

detail of her face. 'I said relax, Cherry. All I have in mind for you this week is hard work.'

That's what he said, that's what she heard. But she also heard the irony in his voice. 'Now why don't you unpack and get changed for dinner? I'll see you in the bar in an hour or so. Don Bennet and his wife are joining us for dinner here tonight, so try not to be any longer, will you?'

But Leon had meant what he'd said about hard work. The following days were the most tantalising, almost tormenting days of her life. They were also interesting—and tiring. At nine on Monday morning they were in the offices of Cooper's architects and by lunch time they were inspecting the site of the brewery with Don Bennet, the head of the firm of architects. Thereafter it was sheer hard work in the offices.

A typewriter had appeared on the writing bureau in Cherry's hotel room and on Wednesday she was confined to her room to transcribe the reams of notes she'd taken from Leon, surrounded by papers, plans, computer drawings, files and folders ... and gardens she would much rather have spent her time in!

But at least it was hot here, so different from the freezing January weather at home! What a run-around she'd had last week, dashing down to the British Airways offices in Victoria to get a cholera vaccination—not because it was compulsory but because Leon advised her to. And there had been a leaving party for Anne on the Friday night—which took up most of the evening. On Saturday, she'd dashed round the shops, buying new clothes suitable for the Kenyan climate, then hurrying home to pack because she and Leon were leaving first thing on Sunday.

When the sun moved to the balcony after lunch, Cherry transferred her typewriter to the table there. Why not work in the sun?

She sat for a while on the lounger, letting her meal digest before starting work again. Of course, it hadn't all been hard work, being here . . . Closing her eyes, she thought of Leon and the hours she'd enjoyed with him during the evenings, of the swimming they'd done together, of the long, leisurely meals they'd enjoyed in the garden restaurant downstairs. And tonight, he'd said, he was taking her out to a bistro, a small, exclusive restaurant where she would have the best food in Nairobi. She knew exactly what she would wear for this date, the white dress with the lace bodice she'd bought in Knightsbridge. And she would wear her hair down.

Her eyes came open and she shielded them against the glare of the sun. She was planning on dressing to please him. Quite what had happened to her during these past few days in Africa, she couldn't be sure, but not only had she relaxed completely in Leon's company, she'd also done a great deal of laughing, had been entertained and enchanted by a man who was so very different from the boss she knew in the office. Keeping her distance, staying aloof, had proved to be impossible for her and when he'd held her hand at the dinner table or put an arm around her as he saw her to her room, she had not drawn away from him.

But that's all he had done, and late last night when he said goodnight at the door to her room, it had taken every ounce of her control not to reach out to him, to invite, to *take* the embraces she was so hungry for. So much for keeping him at arms' length! The only problem she'd had was in preventing herself from taking the initiative!

She dressed with a great deal of care that evening. Everything was just right, her hair, her perfume, her make-up, the accessories to a dress which managed to be both pretty and sophisticated at the same time.

Leon's gaze swept appreciatively over her when she opened her door to him. He took her hands, holding her at a distance so he could look her over from top to toe. 'Beautiful! Cherry, you're a very beautiful woman.'

Cherry's heart jumped crazily, uncontrollably. This was the first compliment he'd ever given her on her appearance—and what a compliment! He'd spoken quietly, intensely, as if to convey that she must never forget his words. Her light-hearted acknowledgement did not come easily. She wanted to look into his eyes and thank him, tell him how very much she cared about his opinion in this and everything else. As it was she just smiled, speaking casually as she reached for her evening bag. 'Why, thank you, kind sir!'

In the intimacy of the restaurant her awareness of him was so acute that she could hardly taste the food she was eating, excellent though it was. Leon had chosen for her, carefully selecting a white wine to accompany their hors d'oeuvre and a different one for their main course.

It was always there, of course, this crackling aura which was the attraction they felt for each other, but tonight the atmosphere was positively throbbing with it. At least, that's how it seemed to Cherry. She had eyes for nothing and no one but Leon, his every move, every smile, every shrug and word, kept her attention riveted on him.

'So what's the verdict?' As they stepped outside into Koinange Street, he was referring to the meal they'd enjoyed, the restaurant itself.

'Superb! Thank you, Leon,' she added quietly. 'It's been a lovely evening.'

They got into the taxi which was taking them back to their hotel, and when Leon reached for her hand her entire body responded to the touch. Every inch of her thrilled to this small embrace as his fingers closed gently around hers.

For minutes they sat like that, in silence, until Leon leaned closer to point out the Kenyatta conference centre to her, his mouth just inches from her face. Her eyes closed briefly, involuntarily. She could concentrate on nothing but him, was waiting and hungry for his kiss . . . a kiss which never came.

It was she who suggested they take a stroll in the hotel gardens, it was she who took over the conversation, chattering about this and that because she didn't want to go to her room, didn't want the evening to end. But it had to end some time, and when Leon saw her to her room, it was she who would stand it no longer, she who did something she'd never have believed herself capable of.

'Leon——' He was walking away, saying goodnight, leaving her bereft, and she simply couldn't let him go! 'Leon, I——'

He stopped, turning to face her as she stood in the doorway to her room, his dark brows raised questioningly. 'Cherry?'

'I want you to kiss me. Kiss me, Leon, please...' She looked up at him as she spoke, her arms sliding around his neck, her breasts brushing lightly against the solid wall of his chest.

He kissed her ... and kissed her ... one long and devastating kiss which served only to make her want more, to make her wish that he would never, ever, stop. She melted against him, her body responding wildly, becoming pliant and inviting in his arms as she moulded her slenderness against the hard contours of his body. For long minutes she had no will of her own, no desire for anything but Leon and the touch of his mouth, his hands.

He drew away, his fingers gripping tightly on her shoulders as he looked down at her with eyes which were aflame with desire, unmasked, unmistakable desire. 'Cherry...' He looked beyond her then, into her room.

She closed her eyes, understanding precisely what he was saying, understanding him now as she'd never understood him before. Leon Silver was a man whose passions ran deep, whose passions were intense, be it in his political views or his zest for life or his hatred or his loves. With him there were no half measures and if he set foot inside her room, the same would apply. It would have to be all or nothing. There would be no turning back . . .

'Goodnight, Leon.' She stepped away from him.

Leon didn't say anything, he merely smiled as he turned and walked away.

He went to his room while he still had the ability, the control, to do so, the control which would be annihilated if he kissed her or touched her again. On his balcony he stood motionless in the black velvet of the night, thinking, smiling at what had just taken place even while he ached with the need for her.

It was business as usual the next day. On Thursday she and Leon were back in the office and their evening was spent as guests at the home of Don Bennet and his wife. They were giving a dinner party for fourteen people and it went on till the early hours.

It was three in the morning when they got back to the hotel and Cherry was falling asleep on her feet. Leon had already told her she could take Friday off, that he'd deal alone with the little work which remained to be done.

Over breakfast on Friday morning, he surprised her by telling her she should pack her bags, that he'd be back at the hotel by lunch time and that they were checking out.

Cherry was half way through a dish of mangoes and paw-paw, fruits she had never tasted until she came to Africa. She'd ordered them for breakfast every morning, loving them. 'But why, Leon?' Her disappointment showed. They weren't due to go back to England until Sunday and she'd secretly hoped he might take her to see the Nairobi National Park on Saturday, that vast area of open countryside through which one could drive and see the animals wandering in their natural environment. 'We're not due to fly home till Sunday evening. Does this mean you want me to change our flights? It's very short notice, I don't think we'll be able——'

'No. We're leaving on Sunday as planned.' He smiled, watching her as she scooped up the last of her fruit. 'But we've earned a rest and there's something you have to see before you leave Kenya.'

'What? Where? And why do we have to check out of this place?' Her disappointment was replaced with curiosity and her eyes lit up. When he said nothing, she grinned at the stubborn look on his face. 'You're not going to tell me, are you?'

His eyes moved down to the provocative swell of her breasts as she leaned forward, pulling a face at him. She was braless, wearing a yellow T-shirt which was embroidered with butterflies and it hugged her like a second skin. He pushed his chair from the table. 'See you later, beautiful girl.'

It gave her something to smile about for the whole morning. Beautiful girl. And where was he taking her? Excited, she went upstairs straight away and packed her suitcase.

She was lying by the swimming pool when he came back just before noon. She was wearing a black bikini which was wet from her swim. Her eyes were closed, but Leon's scrutiny was something she sensed before she actually saw him, before his shadow fell over her where she lay, and she opened her eyes to find his gaze moving slowly over her. 'Oh, I—didn't think you'd be back till one or so.'

'Now that's something in black which really suits you. There's so little of it to give offence. On the contrary . . . Do you plan on travelling in it?' He said it as though he meant it.

'Certainly not! I'd be arrested.'

'I find it very arresting.'

She laughed, covering herself with a towel as she shifted to a sitting position. 'I am ready, believe it or not. All I have to do is throw on some clothes.'

An hour later she was climbing into a white convertible Mercedes. Leon was at the wheel and their suitcases were in the boot. 'This is a lovely car, Leon! Have you hired it?'

'No, it's on loan from Don Bennet. I told him where we were going and he insisted on lending it to me. Nice of him, wasn't it?'

'Very.' There was no point in asking where he was taking her. When Leon Silver made up his mind about something, he made up his mind.

Instead she relaxed in the comfort of the car, her hair blowing in the wind as they drove out into the country on roads which were more civilised than she'd have expected. It was a wonderful, fascinating drive through vast open spaces which were succeeded by the fruit growing areas. They were heading north, getting nearer and nearer the equator and at length Leon pulled off the road and took the approach to a hotel by the Solio Game Reserve where lion, cheetah, leopards and rhino can be seen.

'This is the Outspan Hotel, we'll stop here for a drink. It's the base for guests visiting the Treetops Hotel. You must have heard of Treetops?'

'Of course!' Cherry was delighted. 'That's where the Queen was staying when she got news of her accession to the throne. It's famous. It's built, literally, on the top of trees, isn't it?'

He nodded. 'Perched forty feet high in the branches of giant cape chestnut trees. Beneath it there's a small lake and salt lick. That's where the animals go to water, you can watch them from the hotel.' He pulled the handbrake on and came round to open the door for her.

'Is that where we're staying? Treetops?'

'No.' He grinned. 'But you can have a look at it on Sunday, on the way back.'

Infuriating, intriguing man! She shrugged as they walked towards the Outspan Hotel ... and then she paused in her tracks, fascinated. Outside the entrance there stood a model, a dummy, of a man who had to be even taller than Leon! And it was so lifelike! Dressed in the full regalia of an African warrior, warpaint and all, it stood with a spear held at arms length, making the most awesome picture!

Leon took hold of her hand as she started walking again, unable to suppress a smile as they came level with the model. He stopped, bidding it good afternoon, keeping his eyes on Cherry as he did so.

When the model returned the greeting, Cherry almost jumped out of her skin, squealing with shock and delight. 'Leon! Leon, he's *real*!'

Leon roared with laughter as she stared at the warrior, and when the black, warpainted face turned to her and gave her a broad wink, he was helpless. He took her arm and led her indoors, laughing for all he was worth.

'Why didn't you warn me?' Cherry was walking in one direction while her head was turned in another, still staring in fascination at the man by the door. 'You might have warned me he's real, Leon!'

'And spoil the fun? Mine and his? Never mind, you only get caught out once. I was caught the first time I came up here.'

Within the hour they were back in the Mercedes, on the road again. It was a glorious, marvellous, happy day, and Cherry's eyes feasted on the scenery, on the mountain clearly visible ahead of them. Visible? It was enormous!

It was Mount Kenya!

And they were driving nearer and nearer to it.

All was revealed when they drove through the perimeter entrance to the place which was to be their home for the week-end. It was the Mount Kenya Safari Club—a place Cherry had heard of once, somewhere, vaguely. She didn't really know anything about it, didn't know that it was a small piece of paradise. She didn't know it then, as they drove past two conical-shaped huts flanked by several trees over which there is the club logo, the sign which bears its name.

The Mount Kenya Safari Club is on the equator, seven thousand feet above sea level on the slopes of Mount Kenya, just six kilometres from the small township of Nanyuki, and in it there is virtually everything there could possibly be for the most varied entertainment and luxurious care of its members and visitors.

'Oh, Leon!' Three times she said this as he explained to her exactly where they were, utterly delighted by what she could see as they drove towards the main building of the Club. It was painted white, a sprawling two-storey building with pink awnings over the upper windows. In front of it there was a sweeping lawn, astonishingly green considering the climate, and, beyond that, a swimming pool, and beyond that, a lake.

'This is just the start of it, Cherry. There's acres of land attached to this place which includes a private air field, a game ranch, a golf course, tennis courts—well, you'll find out for yourself. Wait here, I'll get the key from reception.'

She waited, not thinking about his last few words. It was only when she realised they were not staying in the main building, that Leon was taking her to one of the individual bungalows she'd seen dotted around the grounds, that she became instantly suspicious.

'Just a minute, Leon.' She put her hand on his arm as he opened the door of the bungalow which was quite a distance from its neighbour, set among trees. 'Am I to understand that we're sharing this place, that you've booked us in——'

'You are.' He was smiling, unperturbed by the thunder in her eyes. 'What's the matter, Cherry? Aren't two bedrooms enough for you?'

'*Two* bedrooms? Oh, well that's——'

'That's what? Different? You can say that again.' One eyebrow rose in sardonic amusement. 'Fear not, Mrs Simson, you don't even have to share a bathroom with me. As you'll see.'

She saw. Luxury, sheer luxury, that's what she saw! There was a beautifully furnished sitting room in which there was a fireplace, the makings of a fire all set, ready to be lit. She saw the two bathrooms complete with sunken baths and snow white towels as thick as rugs. She also saw the two bedrooms, and was given her choice of them . . .

# CHAPTER NINE

AFTER unpacking she took a long soak in the bath, glad to be out of the car, much as she'd enjoyed being in it. What a place this was! And there was so much to do. Or one could do nothing at all. The choice was simple as that. Given her way, she would opt for the latter. All she wanted to do this week-end was to wander around the grounds, look at the lake, take a swim in the pool, eat and be waited on!

She joined Leon in the sitting room when she'd finished dressing for dinner.

'Is everything to your satisfaction, madam?' he smiled. Her dress was deep blue, almost the colour of her eyes, and it was made from a silky material which had a sheen to it. The soft folds of the skirt swung slightly as she walked into the room and its close-fitting bodice accentuated the gentle curve of breasts whose beauty he had not yet seen. Already, already his desire for her was stirring in his loins! All he had to do was look at her . . .

They ate in the main dining room of the club house, a delicious meal of smoked salmon, fresh lobster, fresh strawberries . . . and it started happening to her all over again. Leon had all her attention, Leon in a dark blue velvet jacket, his white dress-shirt making a contrast against the tan of his skin. Leon, so big and broad and—unspeakably desirable! Leon, Leon, Leon!

She would have to be so careful! She must remember the vow she'd made and keep up her guard.

'Cherry, is something wrong? You've vanished into your own thoughts.'

'No, nothing's wrong. Everything's perfect.'

Leon excused himself for a moment and she slipped

back into her thoughts, glancing round the restaurant. It was so beautiful here, what with the setting, the tropical plants and flowers, the lighting . . . and the man she was with. There was danger in the air. She must *not* forget her resolve, must not forget that there was already a woman in Leon's life.

They strolled back to the bungalow a while later, walking slowly under a starlit sky from which a shimmering moon watched over them. Leon's arm was around her waist, creating a tension inside her, a tension that had been building all evening . . .

She shivered, for the night air was not as warm as she'd expected it to be, and Leon stopped, his arm tightening around her. 'Cold, darling?'

Darling! Oh, if only he meant it!

She pretended he did, she told herself he meant it as he took her in his arms and his mouth hungrily possessed hers.

He kissed her passionately, long and deep. 'I want you, Cherry.' His lips trailed a path of fire from her mouth to the base of her throat, drawing from her a soft moan which came involuntarily.

As they approached their bungalow, the door opened and a waiter emerged, bowing courteously as he bade them goodnight.

When Cherry stepped into the sitting room, all her suspicions were resurrected and alarm bells started clanging in her head. The lamps were on, the fire was lit, adding a warm and romantic glow to the room— and by the sofa there was an ice bucket hugging a bottle of champagne . . .

The air was thick with danger now, and there was only one way she could cope with this. 'Leon——'

She got no further. He drew her into his arms the moment the door was closed behind him, murmuring against the silky skin of her neck. 'Cherry, my beautiful, darling girl . . .'

She bristled, pulling away from him because she had

seen everything clearly when she'd walked into this room, including the falseness of his endearments! 'Stop it, Leon. This has to stop. *Now*.'

Very quietly, he said, 'What are you talking about? What are you afraid of, Cherry?'

'You know what I'm talking about. And I'm not afraid of anything. It's just—this isn't what I want.'

He said nothing, nothing at all. He simply moved away from her and opened the bottle of champagne. He filled two glasses and carried one over to her, his fingers touching hers as he put the glass in her hand. The brief contact sent a tremor through her and her violet eyes went directly to his.

It was only when he sat down, long seconds later, that he spoke. 'Sit down, Cherry. And don't lie to me. Don't lie when every touch, every look that passes between us tells me otherwise.'

'I'm not lying! I—look, we'll go back to Nairobi first thing in the morning, if you——'

'If I what?'

'If you don't want to stay here on *my* terms!'

'Terms?' He seemed to be amused. '*Your terms?* I don't recall terms having been set—by anyone.'

He was laughing now, actually laughing, and she couldn't believe it! She wasn't in the least amused. She was angry! 'I'll say this for you, Leon, you've got style!' She looked around the room, at the fire, at the lamps, at the untouched glass of champagne in her hand. He certainly did have style! He'd set the scene for seduction and he'd done it magnificently, with such finesse, as only a rich and experienced man knows how! 'But all this makes a mockery of your booking a place with two bedrooms, wouldn't you say? Or was that just to put me at my ease? Come into my parlour! How stupid, how innocent do you think I am? It's all too obvious what you have in mind for me here!'

'Here?' He wasn't in the least put out. He was still smiling, though the laughter had gone from his eyes. 'I think you neither stupid nor innocent. As to your next statement—you know exactly what I have in mind for you. I've just told you I want you. But I don't see what difference our surroundings make. Perhaps you'll tell me? I mean, are you or are you not the girl who asked me in a brightly lit hotel corridor to kiss her the other night?'

She looked away. What could she say to that? She had wanted him to kiss her and she'd asked him to. 'I—see. So that's it. I'm afraid you misunderstood——'

He got up then, crossing the room slowly until he stood facing her. 'Misunderstood, Cherry?'

She didn't look at him. Her eyes were on the glass in her hand. He was only inches away, towering over her, and though it was the last thing she wanted to feel right now, she was affected by his nearness, very much so . . .

He didn't kiss her. With two fingers he traced the outline of her cheeks, her lips, her neck. 'Feeling cold again, Cherry? You're trembling . . .' His voice mocked her, compelling her to look at him. 'My dear Mrs Simson, you know as well as I that I could take you here and now. Here, or anywhere else we might happen to be. I have that power.'

Her breath jerked into her lungs as his fingers continued their path, trailing lightly over the bare skin of her shoulders. He was right. He had that power.

'Leon, stop that. Please!'

'*More* games, Cherry? You know, I'm a patient man, but your little game of blowing hot and then cold is beginning to pall.'

'I don't know what you mean! I'm not playing games!'

His fingers moved on, down to the swell of her breasts in the low neckline of her dress. Very lightly he touched her, trailing his fingers over the soft curves. But Leon's eyes were on her face, watching her reactions, seeing her inability to move even as he saw the alarm in her eyes. The compliance of her mind was what he wanted. Not just her body—he had that—but of her *mind*. That's what he was waiting for.

'If you're not playing games, then you're reluctant for some other reason. What is it? You want me, why deny it? Why deny me? Why deny yourself? What is it about you that just doesn't add up? I don't understand you.'

Oh, it was so simple for him, to him! As far as he was concerned they were man and woman and they wanted each other. That's all there was to it. Wasn't that just like a man! But—maybe it would be that straightforward to her, too, if she didn't love him, if all she felt for him was physical attraction.

She brushed his hand away. 'No, you don't understand me. I—goodnight, Leon.'

She escaped into her room, his name on her lips as she lay down fully clothed on the bed, her inner turmoil making it impossible for her to do anything at all. She was very close to tears and she closed her eyes tightly against them.

She thought of David, but only so she could compare him with Leon. The physical attraction she had felt for David was nothing compared to this ... this awful, gnawing *ache* she was experiencing for the man in the next room, the man she loved. She wanted so much to go back to him. She wanted to go to his room and knock on his door and hold out her arms to him.

Putting her fingers to her temples, she fought against the threatening tears and struggled desperately with the dictates of her heart and body versus the intelligence, the common sense which told her to stay where she was.

There were so many conflicting arguments! Why not take what Leon had to offer and simply enjoy it? As he'd said, why deny them both that pleasure?

But what of the future? If only that weren't so plain to see! If only she could believe there might *be* a future with him. But why waste time with daydreams? If she allowed herself to take what she wanted, what he wanted, they would have an affair which would simply fizzle out in time, an affair which would be for him one of many, and for her, eventual heartbreak.

No, *no*, she had protected herself for so long from anything which might hurt her; she couldn't go through it again—loving and losing. To have an affair with Leon would lead to the destruction of everything, her job as his secretary included. For how could she work with him when he moved on to his next woman? It would all turn horribly sour, everything she had now would be lost. And what did she have? She had herself, she had the new life she'd built for herself after years of loneliness and unhappiness. She was not going to destroy it all for the sake of a transitory pleasure.

Cherry climbed out of the water and stretched out on a sun lounger, leaving the pool to Leon, who had far more stamina than she. It was almost lunch time. During the morning, they had driven through the game ranch which is a transit centre for wild game on translocation to other parks and zoos. Of course they'd had to put the hood up on the car—and they'd had to stay *in* the car for safety's sake—and it had been wonderful! She had seen the animals, at last!

'Hungry, Cherry?'

She opened her eyes to look at him, so tall and bronzed, with a physique which conjured up all sorts of images for her if she allowed herself to dwell on the sight of him. The mass of dark hair on his chest was wet, his long and muscular legs set apart as he stood over her, laughing while he shook droplets of water on her. She didn't mind in the least; it was so hot here, absolutely scorching, yet in the distance the two peaks of Mount Kenya, Batian and Nelion, were capped with glistening white snow.

'I'm famished! Oh, Leon, look! Look! Your shadow—you have no shadow!'

'Perhaps I don't really exist?'

She grinned at him. 'No such luck.'

'Thank you very much.'

'Of course!' She snapped her fingers, suddenly inspired. They were on the equator, the sun was immediately overhead and—for a short time at least—nothing and nobody cast a shadow.

'Oh, Leon, look!' She was saying it again when they went in to lunch. They were in the terrace restaurant where a buffet luncheon was being served, but this was a buffet with a difference! There was every type of salad Cherry had ever heard of and many she hadn't heard of. There was seafood, game, smoked salmon and steaks which were being cooked over charcoal to one's preference. The presentation of the food was an art in itself, and in the centre of the main table there was a carving of a ram which looked for all the world as though it were made from ice.

'It can't be, I realise that much! But what is it made of?' Cherry was fascinated, inspecting it closely and deciding it was made from something edible. Leon suggested marzipan but she rejected the idea. One of the waiters settled the argument; it was carved from butter! It was the handiwork of one of the chefs and was kept in cold storage and brought out to grace the table at lunch times.

They took their food on to the shaded terrace and ate leisurely, drinking chilled white wine and chatting about the drive they'd taken. 'Cherry, look . . .' It was Leon's turn now. He was pointing towards the gardens below them and there in all its splendour was a peacock with his feathers spread in a glorious array of colour. He wasn't strutting, he was standing obligingly still, and Cherry lamented not for the first time that she hadn't brought her camera with her.

'Oh, for a camera! Just look at that! How often does one see that? I mean, they never do it when you want them to, do they?'

Leon was enjoying the sight of her, the seriousness with which she made the protest. 'You shall have a camera immediately we've finished lunch. But I don't think the peacock will keep still that long!'

The peacock did not, of course! But there were plenty of other things to photograph, the scenery, the mountain, the lake with its little islands of gaily coloured flowers and its swans. Cherry was in her element, thinking this the most beautiful day of her life. Late in the afternoon there appeared as if from nowhere a flock of pink flamingoes, the delicacy of their colour making her squeal with delight. A little later, just as the sun began its descent, a man with a wheelbarrow sauntered across the lawns, down to the lake. In no time at all he was being followed by birds of every description as he scooped handfuls of food from the barrow, which he scattered around for his faithful entourage.

'Now there's a popular man! Look at them, following him like the Pied Piper!' She turned laughingly to Leon, only to find that his eyes were on her and he was watching her with a concentration she'd never seen before. His eyes were talking to her, whether he knew it or not. They were hungry for her, lit with a desire she had done nothing to provoke.

A ripple of excitement shot through her in response to him, though she looked away, seemingly unaware. 'I—suppose I should go back to the bungalow. I want to have a rest before dinner and to wash my hair.'

'It looks beautiful as it is. Besides, you can't go just yet, there's something else you have to see.'

Again, there was no information forthcoming. He took her into the bar and ordered cocktails. The outside of the bar itself was covered with zebra skins, the tables were circular and shaped like drums, also covered with skins and glass-topped. But she had been in this room before, had inspected with interest the masks on its walls, the trophies, the unusual plants and flowers.

'What is it I have to see in here?' They were on their second drink when she asked the question, at a loss to imagine what it might be.

Leon checked his watch, grinning. 'Any minute now, darling. Be patient.'

Darling. There it was again! And this time it had come spontaneously, naturally, as though he really did mean it. But she mustn't——

All thoughts were swept from her mind when the drummers arrived. Quite suddenly they appeared, running up the lawn in the gathering dusk to play outside the vast picture windows of the bar, the sound of their drums getting louder and louder . . .

'Oh, Leon, how wonderful! What—who are they?'

'The Chuka Drummers. They're part of the Meru tribe who lived on the mountain side in an old area called Chuka. Now sit back and just let their music wash over you.'

Wash over her? She was spellbound, looking through the glass at their black, painted faces, their grass skirts and head-dresses! They were so serious, so intense, and their drumming didn't wash over her, it got right inside her blood, her excitement mounting as the beat got faster and faster, drumming, thrumming, throbbing, to a pitch which kept her almost hypnotised.

It was a wonderful display, something she had never seen the likes of before. Oh, but wasn't that true of everything around here! She felt as though she'd been brought to a different world, a world of beauty, colour, sunshine and music.

Half an hour later she went back to the bungalow alone, almost skipping with delight. Her tiredness had vanished—but she simply had to do something about her appearance. Leon had elected to stay in the bar, insisting he was not going to wait around while she did unnecessary things to her hair.

The flame-coloured dress was lying on her bed and it stopped her in her tracks. Beside it there was a note which was written in Leon's bold handwriting, saying, 'Wear this for me tonight. And no arguments.'

She smiled, trailing her fingers over the pure silk

garment she'd admired earlier in the gift shop. She hadn't bought it, or even thought of buying it, because it was too expensive. Ah, but it was just her colour, a gaily coloured wrap-around style on a flame background.

Her first instinct, however, was a protest. How thoughtful of him it was to surprise her like this—but she shouldn't accept it. They had argued when he bought her the camera. She had insisted on paying for it herself but he wouldn't hear of it.

'Wear this for me tonight. And no arguments.' While bathing, she smiled at the command in his note. She'd better wear it! But . . . but it didn't seem right, accepting gifts from him. It smacked of . . . but she wasn't his mistress, so why should this make her feel like one? Still, mistresses were given presents, weren't they? And taken away for week-ends . . .

She was in the sitting room when Leon came back, which was rather quicker than she'd expected. She wasn't dressed yet, she was wearing only a white satin dressing gown and was brushing her hair by the fire.

'Leon!' She looked up, startled. 'I was—was just drying my hair. I didn't expect you back so soon——'

'I got bored without you.' She was sitting on the floor by the hearth and he sat on the settee, near enough so he could touch her hair. 'You look beautiful like that.'

She doubted it. Her hair was almost dry but it needed taming. She had not long been out of the bath and she had no make-up on, but Leon was looking at her as though he meant what he'd said. 'I—er—about the dress.' It wasn't easy to concentrate. He was trailing his fingers through her hair, playing with it as though it held a fascination for him. 'Leon, I don't think——'

Then she wasn't thinking anything at all. As she turned to make her protest, he caught her face between his hands and his lips met hers before she could utter another sound. She didn't draw away. There was no passion in the kiss, just a sweetness which was intoxicating, a tenderness quite unlike anything she had experienced with him before.

She responded tenderly, all her love for him pouring forth in the gentle touch of her hands as she linked her fingers into the thickness of his hair. She was kneeling, then suddenly she was trying to get away from him as his kiss parted her lips and his tongue began an exploration of her mouth. But Leon's arms came tightly around her, forbidding her freedom. She wrenched her head away, afraid of her own swift arousal. 'Leon, no——'

The effect he had on her was dynamic, instantaneous, evoking a response from her body which she denied with her mind. Her next protest was cut off as he kissed her again, hungrily this time, and with one easy movement he lifted her on to his lap so that she was half lying across him.

She struggled to no avail. On the contrary it made matters worse because the movement parted her gown, revealing the tanned length of her legs. 'Leon! Leon, please——'

He didn't seem to hear her. His lips moved from her mouth to her throat and then he was parting her gown at the top, holding her tightly with one arm as he paused to look at her—just look at her.

She felt the strength seeping out of her, was both frightened and excited by what she could see in his eyes. He was looking at her body as though a woman's nakedness were something new to him.

'Dear God, you are so beautiful! So beautiful!' And then his lips were on her shoulders, inching slowly down to the soft swell of her breasts and Cherry gasped with the shocking pleasure of it as his mouth closed over the taut peaks. Her arms locked around him and she was urging him closer, wanting him never to stop as he gave all his attentions to her breasts, teasing, sucking, taunting.

But *she* would stop. And in a moment she would stop

him because she couldn't cope with this. This was more
than she could tolerate, an ecstasy which must stop here
and now, before she experienced more, before she lost
control.

He was kissing her again, his hands taking over
where his lips had left off, and he was kissing her now
as though there were no tomorrow, in a frenzy of
passion she tried desperately to break away from. And
yet ... and yet she was touching him in return. Her
hands had moved of their own volition inside his shirt
and were exploring the hard contours of his chest,
trailing along the dark hair and then holding him
tightly when suddenly she arched against him. 'Oh,
heaven help me, *no*. Leon, *no!*'

He was groaning, murmuring over and over how
much he wanted her, needed her, and his hand was on
her thighs, moving dangerously closer to that most
intimate part of her. But he had heard her protest. His
eyes were hooded as they looked down at her, drugged
with desire for her, and his voice was barely audible.
'Enough is enough, Cherry.' And with that he closed
both arms around her and stood, carrying her as
though she weighed nothing at all.

Had he not kissed her again as he carried her to her
room, she might have escaped him. She might have. But
the onslaught of his mouth prevented any further
protests, and the fire he had created in her made such
protests less and less desirable. He laid her on her bed
and without taking his arms from her he stretched out
beside her.

Her thoughts were coming in patches now. One
minute there was just the blackness of her closed
eyelids, the mindlessness which was the pleasure of
feeling Leon's strong, hard body against hers and the
next minute there was sanity, the memory of Heidi
Reynolds and maybe several others.

He almost won. It was only when he shifted to undo
his belt that Cherry had seconds in which to pull herself

together, to see what was happening, how very far things had gone. Dear God, if she didn't stop now, she would never stop, she would never be able to! With a sob, she pulled her gown over her nakedness, shouting at him in her need to make him realise she meant what she was saying. 'Get out of here, Leon. Leave me alone! I don't want this—I *told* you! Please!'

And still he kissed her! He gathered her into his arms and held her crushingly close against the hardness of his chest, unable to believe, unable to accept what he had heard.

Cherry went rigid as a new fear crept into her heart. Tears coursed down her face as disillusionment swept over her. He wouldn't—surely he wouldn't just *take* what he wanted? For heaven's sake, how much had he had to drink that he could behave like this?

She gasped, crying in earnest as he raised his head to look at her through eyes which were too bright, too distracted, too ... And then they changed. In an instant she saw recognition in them, recognition and then—and then she saw a fury which was so immense she couldn't bear to look at him any longer. She turned her head into the pillow, stiffening as she heard him swear violently under his breath.

A moment later the bedroom door was slammed shut and she lay motionless, knowing she would never be able to face him again. Enough was enough, he'd said. He was wrong there. Enough would have been too much for her! But for him—she felt ashamed because she'd let things go so far. She should have stopped him long ago, long ago, because Leon Silver was not taking kindly to this, and all she wanted to do at that moment was to curl up and die.

When she heard the outer door of the bungalow slam shut, she gave vent fully to her tears, sobbing against the pillow as though it were all her fault. But it wasn't, it wasn't! She had tried to stop him but he'd been like a man possessed!

It was hours later—one, two or three, she couldn't say—when she heard the door open and close. She was still in her room, sitting by the window like one who was ill, her gown wrapped tightly around her, her hair in total disarray. She didn't go to him. She didn't want to see him, didn't want to talk to him.

But Leon wanted to talk to her. She shuddered as his voice boomed loudly at her from the other side of the door. 'Cherry? Come here, I want to talk to you!'

Her door was locked. She was safe. She didn't respond. His anger had not worn off. On the contrary, it was unmistakable! Had he been back to the bar?

There followed one loud and reverberating thud on her door which had her on her feet before she realised it. 'Cherry! Get in here this minute or I'll break this bloody door down!'

She moved, quickly, a mixture of anger and trepidation rushing through her as she flung open the door. 'How dare you! If you're looking for an apology, you'll be disappointed. You owe *me* an apology, Leon Silver, and if it's not forthcoming, you can go to hell!'

To her amazement, he simply roared with laughter. He took hold of her arm in a no-nonsense grip and steered her towards a chair. 'Sit down, little one. My patience with you has worn down to its last thread, bear that in mind.'

She did. She watched him as he poured a drink from the bottle of whisky which had appeared on the table. It was very difficult to assess his mood from then on. His anger was real enough but it was interspersed one minute with an icy control and the next minute with an impatience bordering on bewilderment.

'Have you been drinking, Leon?' She spoke quietly, aware that she must tread very carefully with him.

'No. I've been walking, thinking. Now then, why the hell didn't you tell me?'

'Tell you what?'

He sat, glaring at her. Then he let out a long breath,

shaking his head as if he couldn't believe what he were about to say. 'That you're a virgin.'

Cherry groaned inwardly, feeling a blush spreading to the very roots of her hair. 'How—why do you say that?'

He seemed now to be exercising enormous patience, with difficulty. 'Because only the uninitiated could have called a halt at the point where you called a halt. If you'd known what it was to be made love to by a man . . . Why the blush? It's nothing to be ashamed of. Astonishing, perhaps, but nothing to be ashamed of.'

'I'm not ashamed.' She was looking at the floor. 'I—I didn't tell you because—because I just didn't see the relevance.'

He slammed his glass down. 'Oh, you didn't see the relevance! Didn't it occur to you that it would help me to understand you better?'

She looked at him blankly. 'No.'

'Well it does. Cherry, for God's sake, you've been married! Why should I have thought for one minute . . . What the devil was wrong with your husband that he never made love to you?'

'Nothing! There was nothing wrong with him. He—I told you he died on our wedding day.'

'You also told me you'd met him six months earlier, that it was a case of love at first sight. So?'

She shifted uncomfortably, not wanting to answer his questions but knowing she'd better. 'It—it was a question of lack of opportunity. Well, it was partly that and partly because of the way I'd been brought up, the morals I'd——'

'Lack of opportunity?' Leon couldn't believe it. 'You got engaged within one week of knowing the man—and you didn't find an opportunity in six months?'

'But I told you David lived with us, with me and my parents. He was Canadian, he joined my father's dental practice straight from university here in England and—and he lived with us as a temporary arrangement at first. Then, well, he just stayed on till we got married. My parents—well, I'd been brought up to believe——' She sighed helplessly and shut up.

Leon didn't say anything else for a long time. He just looked at her, shaking his head. He seemed utterly frustrated with her in a way which had nothing to do with sexual tension. 'Go and get dressed,' he said at length. 'Don't look at me like that, I'll have no arguments from you. We're going to have something to eat before we pack our cases.' He ran his fingers through the thick mane of his hair, muttering half to himself. 'What am I going to do about you, Cherry? What the hell am I going to do?'

# CHAPTER TEN

SLEET was slashing against the bedroom window, melting the instant it touched the glass. The little house in Hampstead was warm but it was freezing outside. It was February, a miserable Monday morning in one of the coldest months of the year. Cherry had been back from Africa for two weeks, two horrible weeks which had left her feeling as though she were living in no man's land.

She pulled on her boots and took her sheepskin coat from the wardrobe, not quite as loath as she had been latterly to go to work because Leon wouldn't be there today. He was spending the day at the factory in Southampton. She would be glad of his absence; it might mean that the atmosphere would be normal for once.

As far as everyone else was concerned, things were running very smoothly indeed in the offices of Silver & Silver. Alec Moore was back in his old routine and so was his secretary, Karen Black.

Karen, normally a very talkative girl, had said little about her broken engagement. She had told Cherry merely that things had not worked out as she'd hoped, that she and her fiancé had discovered they were not right for each other.

Cherry knew the feeling only too well. It was obvious to her that Karen was still suffering over it—something else Cherry could sympathise with, because she was suffering in a similar way. The relationship she'd had with Leon had disintegrated totally. They communicated but they didn't reach one another. During the past fortnight she had on two occasions acted as hostess to dinner parties in the penthouse; they had been entertaining overseas visitors both times and the evenings had gone well. Ever the gentleman—or responsible employer—Leon had taken her home afterwards, but he'd said very little and he had not stepped foot inside her house.

She'd long since given up trying to reach him. For the first couple of days back in the office, she had tried to. She'd been perfectly natural with him, but his mood had been such that she'd given in to the safety of that old economy of conversation.

How much longer she would be able to stand this, she didn't know, because she loved him more than ever. Discovering in Africa the different facets of his personality, his sense of humour, his sense of fun, his appreciation of life and the wonders and beauties it held, had deepened her love to the extent that life with him now was almost unbearably frustrating and depressing.

But life without him was unthinkable.

There had been one hour, just one hour last Friday when she'd thought that their closeness was going to be recaptured. He had come into her office with his children, after having collected them from school, and they'd all had tea together. But even that, she'd learned from the twins, had been at their instigation. They had asked to see Cherry because they wanted to invite her to their birthday party a week on Saturday.

The party was to be held at the family home in Buckinghamshire, and Cherry very much wanted to go but she hadn't given the girls a definite answer. She felt guilty about that, but her acceptance of their invitation depended so much on Leon's attitude towards the idea that she'd hedged. She'd told them she would let them know, that she might have to be in Wales at the time of their party. She had explained to them, truthfully, that her sister-in-law was soon to have a baby and that after the baby's birth, she was going to Wales for a week to help out.

When she'd told Leon this, when she'd asked for a week's holiday, he'd merely nodded his agreement.

And she still didn't know his reaction to the twins' invitation to her. He had taken the girls upstairs after tea—and he hadn't come back to the office. Tomorrow, when she had a moment's privacy with him, she would find out whether he wanted her to go or not.

'Cherry, can you spare me a minute, please?' Alec Moore stuck his head round the door just ten minutes after she'd got to work. She got up at once.

'Good morning, Alec. Of course I can. Penny, would you look after the switch for a while?'

She thought herself lucky to get on so well with her colleagues. There was little she wouldn't do for Alec, he was such a nice man. And Penny Davies was an enormous help, she had mastered her job extremely well and was virtually as capable as Cherry in most respects.

As she followed Alec into his office, the thought crossed her mind that if she had to leave the company, Leon would have Penny to fall back on until he found a suitable replacement. And he would need a replacement. Capable though Penny was, she did lack the experience and sophistication which was necessary for certain aspects of the job as secretary to the MD and Chairman.

'This is very short notice, I know,' Alec said as he waved her into a chair, 'but I need a favour.'

'Fire away. I'll help if I can.'

'Well, I've been let down by someone. I have to attend a dinner do tonight. It's a charity thing, you know, and I need an escort.'

Cherry's first instinct was to say no. This had nothing to do with business and—and what the hell? 'I'll be glad to go with you Alec.'

'You will?' Alec had expected a negative and it was all he could do to prevent himself from grinning. Quite what had gone on between Leon Silver and Cherry Simson, he didn't know, but the former had been like a bear with a sore head since he'd come back from Africa. Quizzing Leon had got him nowhere at all, and it would no doubt be the same if he asked questions of his secretary. *His* secretary! Why the devil hadn't he taken Karen on and left Cherry in her own job? Karen would have coped splendidly working for the MD, but Leon had given him virtually no say in the matter, actually, the way he'd presented his stealing Cherry as the only common-sense solution—more like a *fait accompli*!

There was something in the air. He'd have thought it romance if Leon were not in such a foul mood these days. As for Cherry—well, that gorgeous smile of hers was a rare sight these days. This night out he was giving her would do her good—though he had a strong feeling, Leon wouldn't like it one little bit. Too bad! 'I—did ask Karen, but she'd already made other arrangements.'

For some obscure reason, that made Cherry feel better about the idea. But why not do Alec this favour? What had she to go home to? It wasn't as if there were anything—or anyone—who needed her attention when she finished work.

In a matter of seconds the date was fixed and she went back to her own office.

She'd been in work only fifteen minutes but, contrary to what she'd thought, Leon's absence was something she felt acutely. Things were just not the same when he wasn't around. She would rather have Leon and an awful atmosphere than no Leon at all. Lord, *why* did she have to fall in love again? And why, why did she have to fall in love with her employer? Working here, there was no escape for her. She couldn't distract herself from her pain in any way at all because, present or absent, Leon's personality surrounded her here—in his office, in the work she was doing for him, in the very air itself.

It was three in the afternoon when Heidi Reynolds

came in and made things very much worse. Both Penny and Cherry looked up as the door to the corridor opened; people normally knocked before walking in, but not this visitor! This person was a tall blonde, an immaculately dressed woman with a regal air about her and a smile on her undeniably beautiful face. She walked into the office as if she owned the entire company . . .

Cherry's stomach gave a sickening lurch. This visitor didn't need to identify herself. Still, she treated the woman with what she hoped was appropriate detachment. 'May I help you? I'm afraid Mr Silver isn't in today. He's at the——'

'I'm aware of that.' Heidi Reynolds' voice was smooth, controlled, and it held just the trace of an accent. 'I'm Mrs Reynolds, Mrs Heidi Reynolds. I believe we've spoken on the telephone.'

For the first time in her life, Cherry knew what it was to feel jealousy. She felt an irrational hatred of the woman, which in itself upset her terribly. What an awful emotion to feel! After all, she couldn't blame Heidi Reynolds for—for *existing*.

'Then what can I do for you, Mrs Reynolds?'

The smile was still on her face. She put her hands on the desk, leaning closer to Cherry so that Penny might not catch her words. 'So you're Cherry Simson, Leon's new secretary.'

It was not a question but Cherry answered as though it were. 'I'm Mr Silver's secretary, yes.' The woman's scrutiny was almost offensive, shaking Cherry's composure visibly. What was this all about? What did she want, exactly? 'Was there something? I mean, since you're aware that Mr Silver isn't in today——'

'Just a message I want you to give him. I happened to be passing so I thought I'd call in and kill two birds with one stone, as the English say.'

'I'm sorry?'

She straightened, looking down her nose at the younger

woman. 'I thought it time you and I met. Leon's mentioned your name to me, so I thought I'd call in and say hello. You're aware that I'm a friend of his?'

Was she ever! 'Yes, Mrs Reynolds, I'm aware of that.' Cherry glanced away, only to find there was a smug smile on the other woman's face when next she spoke.

'About that message—just tell him I've been called away on business again, that I'll be back in a few days and I'll ring him this week-end. Goodbye, Mrs Simson.'

As soon as she heard the lift descending, Cherry left the office and escaped to the ladies' room. Even Penny had thought it a strange encounter. She'd turned immediately to Cherry and asked what it was all about.

She might well. Cherry stuck her hands under the cold tap and splashed water on her face. She was flushed and burning inwardly with anger and loathing. What on earth *had* Heidi Reynolds' visit been about? It felt very much as though she'd called in merely to give her lover's new secretary the once-over! Of course there was no evidence for that, and Cherry would be hard pressed to complain of it to Leon. No, she had to forget the idea; he'd think her crazy—or jealous—and that was the last thing she wanted.

Leon didn't react when he was given the message. At nine on Tuesday morning Cherry delivered it coolly and with apparent impartiality, and he merely shrugged as if it were unimportant to him. It was so careless a reaction that Cherry found herself wondering whether it *were* unimportant to him. She still didn't know how serious his relationship with the older woman was—but she was damned if she'd ask! It was still a continuing affair and that was all she needed to know.

'Just a minute.' His voice halted her as she was about to leave his office. He took an envelope from his desk drawer and handed it to her. 'Ronnie and Rachael wrote their party invitations during the week-end. They asked me to give this to you—so it's now official.'

'Yes, I——' she faltered, looking down at the childish handwriting on the pink envelope. 'I wanted to have a word with you about this.'

'You're not going to let them down, I hope?' There was sharpness in his voice but at least it seemed he was in favour of her going to his children's party.

'Well—I don't want to, no. I'm very fond of the girls and I'm flattered that they've asked me.'

'They like you very much, Cherry.'

Something in his voice made her look at him. 'Can I take it then that you won't mind my going to the party?'

'Mind? I want you to. Cherry——'

'Then it's settled. I'd like to tell them myself, can I ring them at their school? After hours, I suppose?'

'Of course. I'll give you the number——'

'I have it. It's in the phone book I inherited from Anne.' She felt suddenly close to tears but she hadn't the faintest idea why. 'Umm—if—if Julie's out of hospital by the time of the party, Mum will spend the week-end in Wales. My brother will——'

'Has she gone into hospital, your sister-in-law?'

'No, she's still at home. The baby's due this Saturday, according to the doctors.'

'Why can't your mother spend more time with her, and what about her own family? Why do you have to take a week off?'

'Julie has no family of her own. My mother can't take a week off just at the moment. She helps my father, she works mornings as his receptionist. Besides, a four-year-old and a new baby would be a bit much for her. She's not getting any younger.'

'But you feel you can cope?'

'I'll love every minute of it.'

'Indeed?' His tone drew her eyes back to his again. 'You're not feeling broody, by any chance?'

'Hardly.' She got to her feet, finding the conversation disturbing. And there had been a good dose of sarcasm in his last question.

'Wait a minute!'

Cherry's hand dropped from the door knob. What had she done now? Why was he suddenly angry—very much so, judging from his tone. Of course! She was making the old mistake of walking out of his office before he'd dismissed her! Damn you, Leon, she thought, there are times when I want to throw myself into your arms and times when I want to run as far away from you as I could possibly get. She turned to look at him and was startled by the glacial green of his eyes. What on earth had she done to upset him now?

'Alec tells me you and he had a date last night.'

'I'd hardly call it a——'

'That you had dinner together at Claridges.'

'Well, yes, but it was hardly a date! I—we weren't alone! It was in aid of charity and——'

'Since when have you felt charitable towards Alec Moore?'

Cherry blinked in confusion. For all the world, it sounded as though Leon were jealous! Surely not? And he was misunderstanding deliberately. Alec must have mentioned what last night's dinner-do was in aid of. Mustn't he? Just in case he'd left room for doubt, Cherry explained, not pausing to remember that she didn't have to justify her actions to Leon or anyone else.

'. . . and the only reason he took me with him was because he'd been let down by some other woman.'

'Did he take you home afterwards?'

'Of course he did.' She saw his face tighten, saw the slight movement of a muscle high in his jaw.

'And did he make a pass at you?'

She was so surprised by the question, so nonplussed at the very idea, she didn't answer fast enough. Before she had a chance to gather her wits, Leon's fist smashed violently against his desk and he got to his feet and grabbed hold of her.

'Answer my question!' He shook her so hard that she

almost lost balance. She stared at him in utter bewilderment.

'Leon, I—let go of me! You're hurting me!' When his fingers bit tighter into her arm, she yelped. '*No!* Of course he didn't make a pass at me! What the devil's the matter with you? Think! Just think about it! Alec's almost as old as my father!'

'So what? He fancies you like mad, always has done. You must be well aware of that!'

She got angry very quickly. She was appalled, at him, at his suggestions, at how very wrong he was. 'I'm aware of no such thing! I don't believe that for one minute! In any case, what business is it of yours? What difference could it make to you?'

He pulled her against him furiously, both hands gripping her painfully by the shoulders. 'I'll tell you what difference it makes to me, I'll tell you what business it is of mine. *I* want you, and that makes it my business! I——' In split seconds his hold on her loosened and he held her very close against his chest, his voice switching from anger to softness just as quickly. '*I* want you. I *want* you.'

Cherry put both hands up and pushed herself away from him. She was at a loss to understand the man. Except for his last remark. '*That,* I am aware of! Now may I please go? Have you quite finished with me?' She turned away, not caring whether he'd finished or not. She'd had quite enough for one day.

'Wait. Please, Cherry . . .' He spoke on a sigh and it was just as effective as his anger in making her obey. She turned, frowning. He'd moved to the window, was standing with his back to her, his hands shoved deep into his pockets. 'Will you spend this evening with me . . .?'

'No, Leon.'

'Why not?' He didn't turn round. 'You spent last evening with Alec, why can't you spend this evening with me?'

'You know why.'

'I said the evening, not the night.'

She bit her lip, her eyes closing against a new threat of tears, not that he was looking at her. Did he think she'd be willing to fill-in until Heidi Reynolds got back at the week-end? *Never!* She hated him for asking her to . . . and she loved him so much that she wanted to say yes, regardless. Lord, what was happening to her? She was constantly at sixes and sevens these days and prone to outbursts of a temper she'd never known she possessed. 'No. In any case, I—I have other arrangements.'

That made him turn round. 'With whom? Alec? Who are you seeing tonight?' he demanded.

'My father,' she said wearily. 'He's coming to some meeting or other and he's taking me to dinner.' And with that, she walked out.

She slumped into her typing chair just as Penny walked in, which made it necessary for her to brighten up, or risk questions from the younger girl. Penny still had a crush on Leon and had complained about his 'odd moods' these days.

There was one consolation, though. Leon must care for her to some extent. His reaction to her having been out with Alec proved that. If only he cared more! If only he cared enough. If only he cared half as much as she did. He'd told her again that he wanted her. So he still wanted her sexually. So what? Was that all he ever had on his mind? She bit thoughtfully on the tip of her pencil. On the other hand, what a flaming nerve he had! How dare he question her movements? She was freer to date other people than he was! And how dare he ask her to spend the evening with him—as a substitute for the blonde!

She felt no anger during the week-end, however. Thoughts of Leon being with Heidi Reynolds evoked nothing but a feeling of nausea borne of jealousy and hopelessness.

On Saturday night she went to the cinema and sat through a film she hardly registered, heard hardly a word of. Visions of two people making love were constantly in her mind until she was almost demented by her own imagination. It wouldn't do, she couldn't go on like this. She would hand in her notice on Monday.

She changed her mind on Sunday. No, she couldn't leave. As things stood, at least she saw Leon every working day. For better or worse. And there was a week in Wales to look forward to. Maybe the break would help her put a different perspective on things. Maybe she'd be able to reach a rational decision then about her future. With luck, she might even start to care less about Leon Silver if she had a whole week away from him.

During the evening, she phoned her brother Kevin to see whether there was any news. There wasn't. The baby was now one day overdue and there wasn't the slightest sign of anything happening.

It was the following Wednesday that her new nephew was born. Kevin phoned her at lunch time, overjoyed, making the usual jokes about cigars and champagne and boys being late.

'Oh, darling, I'm delighted!' Cherry was almost tearful. 'Congratulations, Kevin! Give my love to Julie and tell her I'll see her ... when will she come out of hospital?'

'Oh, they don't keep you hanging about these days!' Kevin laughed, clearly feeling on top of the world. 'She'll be home on Friday.'

'Good grief! That is quick! Er—you know I'm going to a party in Buckinghamshire on Saturday? Mr Silver's children, remember?'

'Yes, yes, you told me. Mind you, it was *Leon's* children when you first mentioned it,' he teased. 'Or are you being overheard?'

Cherry was alone in her office, actually, but she didn't tell her brother that. 'That's right. So cut it out, please.' Teasing about Leon Silver was one thing she didn't need right now. 'Anyhow, I'll come to you afterwards, expect me sometime during the evening. It'll be fairly late, probably.'

'Don't worry, Sis. In fact, come on Sunday if that's easier for you. Mum and Dad are coming on Friday evening and they're staying till Sunday, so no sweat.'

'Kevin, for someone who teaches English you use the most appalling expressions. See you when I see you. 'Bye.'

'Who uses the most appalling expressions?' Leon walked in just as she hung up.

'Kevin. My brother.'

'There's news?'

'The baby was born forty minutes ago. It's a boy. Kevin's delighted, of course, though he wanted a girl, really. He has one son already.'

An odd expression flitted across Leon's face. 'I should think he is delighted. Congratulate him for me when you see him. I envy him his sons . . .'

Cherry looked up quickly. She had no doubt at all about Leon's love for his daughters but, well, he was the last in a very long line of Silver men. 'You—you'd have liked a son, Leon?'

'Wouldn't every man? But I have time, there's no need for you to put it in that tense. Perhaps my next wife will oblige.'

He dropped some files on her desk and walked back into his own office without another word. Cherry's eyes trailed to the closed door and she bit hard on her lip. She remembered, now, his telling her he had every intention of remarrying . . .

# CHAPTER ELEVEN

'OF course, had the girls been born a couple of days later, they wouldn't be Aquarian, they'd be Piscean. Like you, Cherry.'

'But—if there really is something in astrology, how come the twins have such different personalities?'

'The Ascendant, my dear! And the Moon! Oh, yes indeed! They were born an hour apart and the Ascendant and the Moon had changed signs by then. Isn't it obvious to you that Ronnie and Rachael have different moons?'

Cherry bit into her cheeks in an effort to prevent a giggle which might seem rude. She was curious about Helena Silver's hobby and she'd read magazine articles on the different signs of the zodiac—but the twins having 'different moons' was by no means obvious! At least, not to her! She didn't know the significance.

Leon's grandmother spent the next ten minutes enlightening her. Well, partially. Some of her impromptu lecture was so technical it went right over Cherry's head. Helena made no allowances for people not knowing what a 'trine' or a 'conjunction' was! Still, she was such a delightful old lady!

'Er—Mrs Silver, perhaps we should go in now? It's almost one-thirty.'

'Is it really? That's probably why I'm hungry. But you must see the stream, Cherry. It's so pretty . . .'

It was pretty cold out here in the gardens, too! But Cherry smiled and nodded her agreement. She had got to the house at noon because Leon had asked her to. There were no other guests who'd been invited early, for lunch; in fact there would be few adults attending the children's birthday party.

She had been greeted by Leon and the twins the moment she'd brought her car to a halt on the sweeping drive outside the house. The Silver family home was quite something. It was very large, very old and very well cared for. It was a home and not merely a house; there were a lot of expensive antiques around and old portraits of the generations of the Silver family, yet it was a lived-in, comfortable place and Cherry had felt at one with it, curiously, as soon as she'd stepped foot in it.

Leon's father and stepmother had given her a very warm welcome and it was they who'd shown her the ground-floor rooms of the house. It was easy to see where Leon got his extraordinary height from. Leon Silver senior was a big man, as broad as his son and nearly as tall. His hair was silver and very thick, brushed straight back from his face. Unlike Leon, he had blue eyes. Like Leon, he had shrewd, all-seeing eyes.

Leon's stepmother was a friendly woman some ten years younger than her husband, and it was she, together with the housekeeper, who had made all the arrangements for the party. The twins' grandparents obviously thought the world of them—though they were equally wrapped up in each other. They'd only been married a year, they'd told Cherry when showing her around their home.

Afterwards, they'd all gathered in the drawing room for pre-lunch drinks and it was then that Grannie had made her entrance. She monopolised Cherry immediately and took her outside to see the vast gardens surrounding the house.

'Oh, yes, it's very pretty!' At the boundary of the land at the back of the house there was a wide stream which was moving at quite a pace. There were two weeping willows on its bank, their branches overhanging the water, and Cherry stood between the trees, smiling at the lady by her side and saying what an idyllic setting this would be for a picnic on a summer afternoon.

Helena Silver smiled and nodded. She looked just as she'd looked that day she'd walked into the office—except for the shopping bags she'd been carrying. Whether it was her habit to put on her sable for a stroll round the grounds, Cherry didn't know, but everyone was entitled to their eccentricities. As for the red hat . . . well, why not? It was chilly out here!

'My dear, I—well, I brought you out here because to tell the truth, I wanted a private word with you.'

Cherry didn't know why, but this came as no surprise to her. 'Yes?'

'Mm. I'd like you to tell me how you're getting on with my grandson these days?'

These days? Why these days? 'Well, I—er—all right. We have a good working relationship.' Even that wasn't the truth, but what else could she say?

Helena Silver looked positively disgusted. 'I'm not interested in that, child! I want to know what happened in Africa, even if it isn't my business.'

'I'm—not sure what you mean.' Cherry felt trapped. She turned, hoping the old lady would take the hint and they'd walk back to the house.

The grip on her arm was astonishingly strong. It stopped her. 'You're in love with him, aren't you?'

'Certainly not! I can't imagine why you——' A strangled sound escaped from her throat. The eyes of Helena Silver showed more shrewdness than Leon's or his father's. And far, far, more wisdom. 'My dear child, what point is there in lying? You can't get away with that, not with me.' Her smile was almost sad. 'He has no idea. You haven't told him. Why ever not?'

Cherry's throat had closed and it was impossible for her to speak. If she tried to, she'd burst into tears.

But Helena Silver waited, understanding the reason for the silence.

'Grannie!'

They both turned, startled by the booming voice which reached them from a distance of several hundred yards where Leon was standing, waving them in. 'Lunch! What the devil are you up to?' And then he moved, fast, in their direction.

Panic-stricken, it was Cherry who grabbed hold of the old lady's arm now. 'Oh, Mrs Silver, *please!* You must respect my——'

'Hush! Of course I will! You don't think I'd interfere in affairs of the heart, do you? Great Scott, do you think I'm mad?'

No, not mad. Well-intentioned and possibly mis-guided, but not mad. Helena Silver was far from that, despite her inconsistent dotty act; as Leon had called it.

'Relax, Cherry,' she said sternly, 'your secret is safe with me, I promise you.'

Cherry believed her. She felt suddenly weak at the knees and it wasn't helped by Leon coming towards them with a thunderous look on his face.

'Don't frown like that, Leon!' His grandmother admonished. 'You'll get lines on your face. Like me!'

'What are you two nattering about that's keeping you from lunch? We're all waiting for you!'

'It's none of your business, but I'll tell you anyway. I was just telling Cherry that the Scorpio man is a character who's often too intense for his own good. He can be extremely rude, extremely moody, and he can bark at little old ladies without even a twinge of conscience or a thought for their frailty.'

'Frailty, my eye! You're as tough as old boots and you're a first class villain.' He took hold of his grandmother's hand and linked it through his arm. 'And I've told you before, I don't want you filling Cherry's head with all that astrological gobbledygook.'

His grandmother sniffed. She withdrew her arm and stuck her nose in the air. 'Take Cherry in to lunch, you overgrown cynic. *I* shall eat in my room.'

And with that, she walked away, leaving Cherry staring after her and Leon looking—well, neither cross nor amused, but a little of each.

'You've really offended her now. I think.' Cherry was uncertain, concerned.

'Rubbish! She's up to something. She didn't by any chance ask you where you were born and what time and what date?'

'No, just—yes!' She started laughing. Helena had elicited all this information but her questions had been interspersed with so much chattering that Cherry hadn't noticed. She was laughing helplessly now. Was it a family trait, this ability to get people to tell things about themselves? Or was it . . . 'Leon, what sign is your grandmother?'

'She's a Scorpio, too. Oh, Cherry!' He started laughing with her, putting an arm around her waist and drawing her close. 'Don't start taking it seriously! All that nonsense about——'

She looked at him impishly, forgetting for the moment all the tension, all her resentment, all her jealousy. 'Oh, yes? And you don't, I suppose?'

'Of course not! Why, you rogue! Come here!' And then he was kissing her and suddenly it wasn't cold any more. If Helena Silver was still in sight—well, that didn't matter. At least they couldn't be seen from the house, not where they were standing.

Seconds later she wasn't worrying about that, either. She wasn't aware of anything but Leon and the hunger in his kiss. She could hardly breathe for the way he was holding her so tightly against him. Gasping for air, gasping with pleasure, she tried to pull away from him when his lips moved to her neck. Did he never give up? If only she could switch off, if only his kiss didn't fire her with uncontrollable yearning for more, more!

'Leon, stop it! Are you crazy?'

There was no laughter now. The grip of his fingers was not cushioned by her coat, they bit tightly into her arms and held her immobile, just inches away from him. There was fire in the intense green of his eyes, a desire he did not, could not, deny.

'No, I'm not crazy. Only for you. But if I don't make love to you very soon I think I will go out of my mind.'

'Let me go, Leon! You're not talking sense!'

'Sense? I love you, Cherry. Does that make sense? Does that make any difference to you?'

'Not one bit! Now let *go* of me!' She turned and she ran.

She ran blindly, hurt and furious by his careless lie. Dear God, he must be desperate to make love to her if he'd go as far as saying he loved her! It wasn't the first time a man had said that to her in an effort to persuade her into something she didn't want to do.

Men! What bastards they could be at times! They seemed to think those three little words were an open sesame with women—no matter how falsely they were spoken.

She went into the house by the back door and spent five minutes in the downstairs loo, trying to regain some semblance of normality before facing the rest of the family and lunch. If Leon only knew how much his lie had hurt her, would he have said what he'd said? She liked to think not, she liked to think he cared enough not to wish to hurt her deliberately. Surely he did care that much?

Over lunch and during the party in the late afternoon, he showed no signs of caring for her at all. He wasn't even as friendly towards her as the rest of his family were. Fortunately there was little conversation between them because there was so much distraction at the party and an enforced silence when a hired magician turned up to entertain the twins and their young guests.

The children had the time of their lives but Cherry's day was ruined. She wanted to leave, was marking time until she could get into her car and head for Wales. Once, fleetingly, she looked up to find that Leon's eyes were on her. They were intense, looking at her as though she were a stranger, and the effect of this was chilling and heartbreakingly sad. His desire was turning to resentment, she was sure of it. Leon Silver was used to getting what he wanted in life. He was a leader, he was in command of a business employing hundreds of people. But he was not in command of her.

And yet he was.

He not only had the power to excite her beyond description, he also had the power to break her heart. And that was just how she felt now. Hadn't she thought that all would eventually turn sour if she had an affair with him? Well, she hadn't had an affair with him, but everything had turned sour nonetheless. Their relationship was in ruins. What bitter irony! She might just as well have given in to him in Africa. She should have lived for the day and taken the pleasures he was only too eager to offer. To hell with love, to hell with Heidi Reynolds, to hell with morals, she should have lived for the day!

There again . . . thank God she hadn't. It would be worse, *worse* if she had expressed her love physically, worse if she'd known what it was to have Leon inside her, a part of her. Leaving him would be all the more painful. And she was going to leave him. She was going to hand her notice in, without fail. She couldn't take any more.

'But we thought you were staying to dinner?' The younger Mrs Silver was quite perplexed when Cherry announced she was going. It was seven in the evening and the last of the children had just been collected by their parents.

'My dear, you can't go!' Grannie seemed very put out. 'I thought you were staying the night!'

Leon didn't help at all. He was sitting in an armchair by the fire, leaving her to it. He wasn't even looking at her. He seemed more interested in the flames of the fire than in anything else.

Embarrassed, Cherry hardly knew what to say. She could have stayed the night. All it would need was a phone call to her brother. But the idea was out of the question. 'No, I—I have to drive to Wales this evening.'

She looked from the old lady to Leon's stepmother. 'I'm so sorry, there's been a misunderstanding.'

Leon still didn't speak.

'Yes, Leon mentioned you were going to Wales. But he told us—Leon?' His father got his attention. 'Help me persuade this charming girl of yours to stay and eat with us! You told us she'd stay to dinner, at least.'

'I thought she would.' He didn't look up. 'But Cherry has been known to change her mind several times over several matters, Dad. Persuasion will have no effect on her. She'll just do as she wishes in the end.'

Looks were exchanged. Only the twins were oblivious. Rachael got hold of Cherry's hand, her pretty face showing all the disappointment she felt. 'You haven't seen our room! Has she, Ronnie?'

'You said you would, Cherry. You said after the party we'd take the presents upstairs and——'

'Of course we will! I'll come and see your room now.' She smiled at the girls and apologised to the others. 'Really, I'm sorry I can't stay for dinner but it's a long drive . . . I—it's been a lovely day. Thank you so much!' She had never felt so awkward in all her life. Damn Leon! He might have told her she was expected to stay for dinner. He always had taken too much for granted . . .

'Oh, my dear, thank *you*.' Mr Silver took her by the hand, changed his mind and kissed her cheek instead.

'It was kind of you to come, Cherry.' His wife did likewise. 'You're really good with children, aren't you?'

'There are some things which come naturally to her.' Leon's voice was so flat, so even, that his deliberate ambiguity was caught by Cherry and nobody else. She ignored it. She ignored him.

'Come on, Cherry . . .' Two hands were tugging at her now.

The old lady had the last word. 'I'd like to show you something before you go, Cherry. I'll be in my room. The girls will show you where it is.'

Leon's grandmother was irresistible. 'All right.'

She went upstairs with the twins, determined that she would not say goodbye to their father. 'Oooh, I say! This is nice! Who chose that wallpaper?'

In a voice that was unbelievably serious, Ronnie said, 'It was a joint decision.'

Cherry swallowed hard. What a silly fool she was! She was in danger of crying again, just because Ronnie had sounded so much like her father—the Chairman of the Board! 'I see. And the curtains?'

The answer was the same.

'You must miss being at home. Do you sleep in a dormitory at school?'

'Yes, but we like being with the other girls. We like school just as much as we like it here.'

'And we like staying at the penthouse, too.'

'Well, you're not difficult to please, are you?'

Everything in their bedroom and bathroom was admired, everything chatted about. They were so sweet, these two little girls with faces which were no longer identical—not to Cherry, who had learned to see the differences, minor though they were. But one couldn't mistake them. Rachael was the chatterbox and Ronnie—she was more serious, like her father. Because of her Moon, no doubt.

She forgot all about her promise to the old lady when there was a sudden, dramatic groan from Rachael.

Cherry was sitting on the bed with the other child, who had asked to see her lipsticks and was now examining the contents of her make-up bag with much fascination. Rachael was by the window, about to close the curtains when she let out the loud groan.

'It's Mrs Reynolds! I thought she couldn't come today.'

Cherry felt the blood draining from her face. 'I—you weren't expecting her?'

'No!' It was a chorus.

She had to leave. Now. Facing Heidi Reynolds was more than she could cope with today. Or any other day.

She never wanted to set eyes on her *or* her lover again.

Ronnie moved to the window and stood by her sister's side. 'She's got presents. She's getting them out of her car.'

'You—you don't sound very pleased, girls.'

'We don't like her! Look, Daddy's gone out to help her. Oh, *bum!*'

'Rachael!'

Rachael turned round, dragging the curtains together. 'I don't care!' she said defiantly. 'We don't like *her!* She's always giving us big presents that cost lots of money. But it makes no difference, does it, Ronnie?'

Ronnie was shaking her head, almost morose. 'And she's going to be our new mother. Daddy's going to marry her. Did you know that, Cherry?'

'I——' It was just as well she was sitting down. Her legs felt as though they'd turned to lead. 'I had an idea. When—when did he tell you that?'

'At Christmas. *She* asked us how we liked the idea of having a new mother.'

'She—Mrs Reynolds spent Christmas here, did she?'

'Yes, worse luck.'

'And Daddy told us that by summer he's going to be married.' The girls looked at each other, shrugging resignedly. 'We'll have to go down, Cherry. She's brought presents and we'll have to go and thank her. If we're rude to her, Daddy will get very cross.'

'Yes, yes, I—can imagine.' Cherry got unsteadily to her feet. She had to pull herself together rapidly. She had to get out of this house without being confronted by Leon or the Reynolds woman, without seeing anyone.

It worked. They were all half way down the stairs when they heard the voices in the drawing room. She turned to the girls, speaking quietly. 'Look, I—won't disturb your father. I've already said my goodbyes. So off you go.' She planted a swift kiss on their upturned faces, then hurried silently across the hall and out the front door.

# CHAPTER TWELVE

SHE drove fast, dangerously fast. She continued like that until she was half way to Wales and she realised what she was doing. Then she stopped the car altogether and stared at the tail lights of the vehicles zipping past her.

Her hands started shaking and she held them together tightly against her mouth, letting her teeth sink into a finger, hoping it might take her mind off the pain in her heart if she created pain somewhere else.

There was nothing, nothing at all left to hope for. Why had she hoped at all? Ever? Why hadn't she seen weeks ago that Leon's interest in her went only as far as her body? Why had she paused just for a second, during lunch, to give a little more thought to what he'd said? Just fleetingly, there had been a moment when she'd wondered whether there might be some truth in his saying he loved her. She'd given it momentary consideration only because she had never before known him to say something he didn't mean. Leon was the type of man who'd say nothing rather than do that.

But she'd quickly dismissed the possibility. And then, later, she had seen the resentment in his eyes ...

Was there no end to her stupidity?

'Yes. It ends now. Right now!' She put the gear lever into first and drove on at a reasonable pace. She wasn't going to risk death because she'd lost someone she'd never had in the first place. Nor would she let this ruin her life. She had been through that once in the past; this time it would be different. She had built her life again after losing David, she would do it again now. She would write her letter of resignation from Wales. There was no question of her giving notice, she had already

174

quit her job. Next week, he'd find out she wasn't going
back. Nothing and no one could induce her to step foot
inside that office block again.

Julie was asleep by the time she got to the house. So
was the new born baby. Her parents and Kevin were
watching the late night film, but they switched the TV
off when Cherry arrived.

'You look tired, Cherry.'

'You look strained. Are you unwell?'

'Why didn't you leave it till tomorrow? It's late, we
all thought you'd decided to stay the night in Bucks.'

She couldn't talk about it. She couldn't tell them
anything. She waved away their questions and told
them laughingly it had been quite a day, what with all
those children and the noise they made. 'Come *on*,
Kevin! Don't keep me waiting any longer. Show me
your new son!'

She and her brother sneaked quietly into his bedroom
where the baby was sleeping. 'Only for the first couple
of weeks, you understand.' Kevin whispered laughingly.
'After that, he's in the nursery where he belongs.'

'Quite right, too.' Julie opened her eyes sleepily.

'Oh, Julie. I'm sorry!' Cherry apologised for the
disturbance. 'I just had to see him straight away. He's
beautiful!'

'Like Kevin.'

Cherry giggled. 'No, not like my brother! The baby's
beautiful. I hope you've decided on a name by now? It's
taken you long enough . . .'

Because her parents were occupying the guest room,
Cherry had to sleep on the settee that night. Not that it
mattered. She didn't sleep at all until the early hours,
and then only briefly, fitfully. But the comfort of a bed
wouldn't have made any difference.

By Monday she was wishing herself elsewhere. It was,
psychologically, quite the wrong place to be. Kevin and
Julie's happiness threw her own misery into sharper
focus. The two of them were as much in love as they

had been the day they married, seven years earlier and the new addition to their family was loved and wanted and ... and if only, *if only!*

They knew something was wrong, very wrong. Much as she busied herself, Cherry was not herself. On Tuesday, Julie came right out with it and Cherry gave up.

'It's Leon Silver, I realise that much. Tell me about it, Cherry, for heaven's sake! I know you're in love with him. I knew it at Christmas.'

'So you did. I ... All I need to say is that at Christmas, when I was discovering how I felt about him, he was proposing to a woman by the name of Heidi Reynolds, someone he'd been seeing for a year.'

'Oh, no! Oh, Cherry!' There was no analysis, no post-mortem. There was no point. The conversation stopped there, and Cherry left the house a few minutes later to fetch Christopher from play school.

Neither Kevin nor her parents mentioned Leon's name to her. Her parents phoned daily and she knew they'd have been told by Julie. She appreciated this. Talking about it would not help, not in this case.

She didn't actually cry about it till Wednesday. The tears came when she got into bed, and she cried for an hour or so. She wanted to go home, didn't want to be here a minute longer. She wanted to be alone. But she had to stay at least until Friday, when her parents were coming. Julie was tired and she needed some help. Besides, it would be unfair to leave because, had she not committed herself to this week, Kevin would have taken time off from the school where he taught. But she'd volunteered to help out, so that was that.

The letter to Leon was still in draft form and was in the bedside drawer in the guest room. How many times had she started it? Five, six, seven? She took it out, blinking against her tears, pulling herself together again. Why worry over the wording? She must finish it, now. If she posted it straight away, he'd get it on

Friday. She ought to have posted it days ago but she'd hesitated, stupidly, over the wording of it.

She picked up her pen and started afresh, and this time she finished it. Plainly and simply she said she was not going back, that this was not her notice but her resignation. She said that during her first few weeks with Silver & Silver, she'd told him she needed six months in which to learn all the aspects of her job, that she'd now had those six months and was not happy with the work.

After reading it through several times, she nodded. It was perfect —straight to the point, no waffle. She signed it and wrote the envelope, marking it personal, for the attention of Leon Silver.

She didn't wait till the morning, didn't want to miss the early collection. If she posted it now, it would be sure to get there on Friday. She pulled on a pair of jeans and a sweater and went out there and then, at midnight, to put it in the letter box.

'Would you get that for me, Cherry? I've just put one foot in the bath!' Julie called down as the phone rang.

It was Friday morning—Cherry got up to answer it. It was her father.

'Hello, darling? How are you?'

'I'm fine, Daddy, just fine.'

There was a pause. 'If you say so. Where's Julie?'

'She's in the bath. Anything wrong? You are coming this evening, aren't you?' She hoped so! The need for privacy had become more and more vital with every passing day, and she was desperate to go back to Hampstead, to the quietness of her own home. And it was her home. At least until the owners came back, which was six months away. She would stay there. She would not go running back to mother, as she had in the past. She would face the world and all its realities and find herself a new job. There was plenty of work in London.

'Actually, we can leave Bristol earlier than we'd thought. I only had two appointments for this afternoon, a married couple, and they've just cancelled. Got the 'flu. So we'll be early, okay?'

'Fine. What time shall we expect you?'

'Well, your mum's just starting lunch ... around three, I suppose. See you then.'

'Er—no, you won't. I think I'll go home after lunch ... Yes, I will drive carefully. All right, Daddy. 'Bye.'

Penny Davies took the lunch-time post from the messenger and looked suspiciously at the white envelope which was marked personal. It had a Welsh postmark on it, not that she needed a clue. She recognised the handwriting. It was from Cherry. Now why should Cherry write a letter to Mr Silver? Why, when she would be seeing him on Monday morning?

'Excuse me, Mr Silver. The second post has just arrived.' Penny put the folder on the desk in front of her boss. She'd opened all the letters except the one from Cherry.

When Mr Silver merely grunted, she went on a little nervously. 'Er—there's one marked personal.'

'All right, Penny. Thank you. Carry on.'

That was his way of telling her to go. She got as far as the door, her unease growing by the second. It gave her courage. 'It—it has a Welsh postmark on it. I—think it's from Cherry.'

Leon looked up from the sheet of figures he was studying but by the time he did so, Penny had gone. 'What?' He picked up the letter.

Two minutes later he was bellowing through to the next office. 'Penny! Come in here! No, stay where you are. Get me directory enquiries. No. Don't bother. Fetch Mr Moore in here. No. Don't do that, I'll buzz him.'

Think man, think! What the hell was this all about? He snatched up the single sheet of paper again and shoved it in his trouser pocket. He didn't need directory enquiries. The address was printed on the paper. 'Damn you, Cherry, I'll sort you out if it's the last thing I do!'

He picked up the internal phone and punched two numbers. 'O'Connell, bring the car round immediately. No, we're not. I don't need you. I'll drive myself.'

He hung up and hit two other numbers. 'Alec? I'm going out and I won't be back. I want you to deal with Robin Long for me, he'll be here at two. No, I'm going to Wales.' He hung up and dialled a number on the external phone.

'Put my father on the line ... Well, who *is* there? Yes, put her on straight away ... Grannie? It's me. When will Dad be back? Right. Ask him to collect the children for me this afternoon. I have to—what? Wrong? *Wrong?* I'll tell you what's *wrong!* I've just got a letter from a certain young woman, the most cold-blooded missive I've ever set eyes on! So much for your advice, eh? Not only did she run away—she's never coming back! Well, that's what she thinks! I'm going to Wales right now and I'll drag her back by the roots of her hair if necessary ... I'm *not* in a foul mood, I'm in a murderous mood. What? What do you *think* I'm going to do about it? No, I am *not* going to ask her to marry me. That's just where you're wrong! ...'

He was on the road four minutes later, cursing himself and cursing the woman he loved.

He was still in the same state almost two hours later, though his fury was directed solely at himself by then. What had happened to him? Had he lost control altogether? Had she actually succeeded in driving him out of his mind? For a decisive man who had handled every blow life had dealt him so far, this was something new, this uncertainty, this feeling that he wasn't sure of anything any more. No. No, it wasn't new. He'd lived with it for weeks.

Where the hell was the map? He'd taken a wrong turning somewhere.

His bark of laughter was hollow. He certainly had taken a wrong turning somewhere—with Cherry. But how, when, where, he simply didn't know. Well, he'd tried everything in his power so far. There was only one solution left.

He pulled over, opened the glove compartment and took out the hefty red book which was the road map of Great Britain. What sort of god-forsaken place did her brother live in? Why couldn't he live in Swansea or Cardiff or somewhere civilised like that?

He closed his eyes briefly, barely able to concentrate on what he was doing, hearing again his grandmother's voice as she'd blasted him over the telephone . . .

'Why, you outsized oaf! Why don't you try *asking* the girl instead of telling her!'

He switched the engine off and tried to calm down. The old darling was probably right. She usually was. He must calm down before he faced Cherry. He must calm down and ask her to marry him instead of telling her she must.

Which is precisely what he would have done, if he hadn't got to Wales and discovered that Cherry was no longer there . . .

# CHAPTER THIRTEEN

THE house in Hampstead was cold. She should have left the central heating on low.

Cherry switched it on and she lit the gas fire, too. Well, she was home. What now? It was almost dark outside and the evening stretched ahead of her, long, unwelcoming and unwelcome. So what now? She didn't even have a newspaper to see what was on the TV. Still, she had to go to the shops in any case. She needed a jar of coffee and some milk and some food for later. She might as well get back in the car and go to the supermarket. She didn't take her coat off, she went out straight away. At least the house would be warm by the time she got back . . .

It was. She shivered against the sudden warmth as she fought her way through the front door, laden with three shopping bags. As usual, she'd bought more than she'd intended to. But her first priority was a cup of tea, she was gasping for a hot drink. She made a pot and took the tray into the living room, and she was just about to close the curtains when she saw the black Rolls come to an abrupt halt outside her door.

Panic-stricken, she dragged the curtains together. 'Leon!' What did he want—a confrontation? She wouldn't let him in . . . but he was already ringing the door bell.

Heavens, what was wrong with the man? It sounded as if he were *leaning* on the door bell. 'Oh, God!' Muttering aloud, she went to the door. There was no point in ignoring this man, he'd stand there all night if necessary—or break the door down. By the sound of it, he was furious with her!

That was an understatement. He walked straight past

her, shedding his overcoat as he did so and flinging it on an armchair. 'I've been halfway across Britain looking for you!' he bellowed, fishing in his trouser pocket. 'What the hell is this supposed to be?'

He was waving her letter at her and Cherry couldn't move, had no idea what to say for the moment. She hadn't expected this reaction! So he'd been to Wales! Why on earth hadn't her family warned her? They might've rung to warn her he was looking for her, might have given her the chance to take evasive action! She'd have gone out if she'd thought for one minute that he'd——

Of course! She had been out. She'd been shopping. Julie had probably tried to ring her . . .

'Don't stand there gaping at me! Answer me!'

*'Calm down!'* She snapped into action at once. 'How dare you come here like this—unannounced, bellowing at me?'

He was furious. The glint in his eyes was a very dangerous one and when he took a step towards her, Cherry took three steps backwards. 'All right, all right, Leon!' She was shouting now, as angry as she was frightened. 'I should have thought it obvious. That's—it's my resignation.'

'I'm well aware of that! But *why?*'

'I told you in the letter. I've had my six months, more or less, and I decided I don't like the work. I—I can't take the pace, which is just what you thought in the beginning. You were right, you see.'

Leon was pacing around the room and he told her in one word what he thought of that explanation.

'Don't use that kind of language in front of me, Leon. It isn't—rubbish. I'm not happy at the office, that's all.'

'Why? *Why?*' He was still shouting—and so was she. 'Why the hell can't you be honest?' he demanded. 'And tell me what's really amiss?'

She faced him squarely, fuming, half-conscious of

what the neighbours must be thinking. This was a terraced house and if they couldn't hear her voice, they'd certainly hear his! 'All right, I will! I'm leaving because I can't stand working with you. Because I can't stand *you*. Because you're an insensitive bully and I hate the sight of you!'

He stopped pacing then. And his hand stopped rubbing at the back of his neck. He shoved both hands into his pockets, visibly relaxing as he stood, smiling at her now. He was just—just smiling as though that were the most amusing thing he'd ever heard! 'Is there any tea in that pot?'

'Get out of here!' She thought him mad, absolutely mad.

But Leon was still smiling. 'Pour me a cup of tea.' And with that he flopped into a chair, grinning broadly as he stuck his feet on the coffee table.

Cherry moved swiftly. She snatched up the teacup and saucer she'd set for herself and flung them at him, one after the other. 'I said get *out* of here, Leon!'

The cup flew straight for his face and bounced off the arm he put up in self-defence. He was roaring with laughter now, *roaring,* and it was more than she could stand . . . And then he was on his feet, moving ever so slowly towards her, still laughing at her behaviour. 'Does this china belong to you?'

Oh, it was too much, too ridiculous! Everything had gone wrong. Everything! Even the saucer had broken. It had hit the fireplace and shattered into a dozen pieces, and no it wasn't her crockery . . . As if that were the biggest tragedy of all, she burst into tears. All the tension, weeks and weeks of pent-up emotion, suddenly surfaced in her and she started sobbing as Leon's arms came around her.

He let her cry, holding her as though she too were made of china. 'It's all right, Cherry. It's all over now. I told you once before, enough is enough.' His voice was gentle now, very quiet and very gentle. 'You don't need to tell me how you really feel . . . but I'd very much like to hear you say it.' He put a hand under her chin, making her look at him.

Cherry felt utterly defeated, exhausted. Her vision was blurred and her tears kept coming, trickling down her cheeks and on to his fingers. 'I love you,' she said simply.

Leon smiled down at her before cradling her head against his shoulder. 'It's just as well you're resigning from your job. If you hadn't, I'd have fired you anyway.'

'Y-you would?'

'Most definitely.' He held her tighter, nuzzling his face against her hair. 'You see, I have another job lined up for you, my darling. As my wife.'

'Your——' She pulled away, staring at him, putting her abnormally cold hands against her abnormally hot face. She felt dizzy, unable to believe what she'd just heard. 'Your—*wife? Me?*'

Leon frowned, uncertainty creeping into his eyes. 'Cherry, you have to marry me, you must! I mean— what I mean is, will you? *Will you?*'

It was Cherry's turn to laugh now, but she gave him his answer quickly because she couldn't bear to see the worry in his eyes. 'Yes. Oh, yes! But——' She shrugged helplessly, laughing and crying again. 'The twins told me you were going to marry Heidi Reynolds!'

'*What?*'

They stared at one another, each expecting an explanation. It was Cherry who pulled herself together first. 'Oh, Leon, pour me a drink. There are some glasses and a bottle of brandy in the cupboard over there. I need something stronger than tea!'

He did as she asked, bombarding her with questions at the same time. She told him quietly and calmly what the children had said. She told him word for word, but it didn't seem to make sense to him.

'But I didn't propose to Heidi at Christmas! Then or

any other time. On Christmas Eve, I *finished* with her. That was when I finally stopped fighting against what had happened to me, when I accepted that I was in love with you and there was nothing in the world I could do to help myself. I knew then that nothing less would do, that you had to be my wife. So I told Heidi there was someone else, that——' He broke off.

'What is it?' There was realisation in his eyes and Cherry wanted to be in on it. 'Leon?'

'Heidi. When I told her it was over between us, she took it well considering . . .

'Considering—what?'

'Considering she'd planned on asking me to marry her.' He got up, obviously disturbed by the memory. 'I had no idea she was in that deeply. In fact I'm not sure she was, actually. She said, "What a pity, Leon. I'd planned on proposing to you tonight. We'd make a good team, you and I." But she was philosophical, to the point of nonchalance, as though she'd been thinking in terms of a merger rather than a marriage.'

'But that doesn't explain the twins saying you'd told them you'd be married by the summer.'

'Cherry, the children *asked me* whether I was going to marry again. I—hell, I just thought it was a question out of the blue, you know what children are like. Then I thought perhaps they'd realised what was happening between you and me. They—Ronnie especially—they're both very perceptive. So I said yes, hopefully by the summer. I couldn't be more specific than that.'

'And when was this? At Christmas?'

'No, no. About two or three weeks later. Yes, it was the day before we left for Kenya. They'd obviously been worrying over the question Heidi had asked them, and they added my answer to it—and came to the wrong conclusion. Grief, I had no idea she'd asked them how they liked the idea of having a new mother! To think they've been worrying all these weeks . . . I'm well aware that they've never liked her . . .'

'I still don't see——' But Cherry did see. Now. She saw a great deal. Heidi's question to the children had been premature, had been asked before she and Leon had talked. She must have been very confident of his accepting her proposal! 'Why—how come she was with you at Christmas?'

'My family were expecting her to dinner on Christmas Eve. I'd invited her several weeks earlier and I saw no reason to put her off. It wasn't as if—anyhow, it was as good a time and place as any to talk to her about you.'

'Did you—I mean, did you tell her you were going to marry me? Did you tell her who this other person was?'

'No, to both questions.' He sat beside her, taking hold of her hands and pressing the palms to his lips. 'How could I? It was all a theory—my theory. I knew what *I* wanted but I didn't know what you wanted. I had no idea how you felt about me.'

But Heidi Reynolds had guessed who the someone else was! Cherry told him of her visit to the office the day he'd been in Southampton. 'She was giving me the once-over, weighing up the opposition! Of course she'd guessed who I was.'

'Well, I had mentioned your name to her several times, in conversation about work, and maybe she just——'

'But how did she know you weren't in that day? And did she ring you that week-end?'

'No. Now don't look at me so dubiously, darling, she didn't ring me. She knew I was going out of town because she'd phoned me in the penthouse that very morning. She'd asked me to meet her for lunch, said she wanted my opinion on a business matter.'

'But you didn't meet her . . . because you were out of town?'

Leon chuckled at that. 'Cherry, I've just told you, I broke off my relationship with her at Christmas. I didn't meet her because I knew damned well she didn't

want to talk business. She's a beautiful woman and
she's well aware of it. What she really wanted was to
find out whether my new affair was still thriving——'

'Or whether there was still a chance for her! Oh,
Leon!' She groaned, her dislike for Heidi Reynolds as
strong as ever. Heidi had deliberately upset her,
deliberately implied she was still seeing Leon—and
Cherry had been only too willing to believe it! 'She
doesn't give up easily, that woman. I suppose that's
why she turned up at your father's house last week. The
children did say they weren't expecting her. Their
birthday was a good excuse for her to see you again,
that's all. She brought them presents and——'

'Darling, she was at the house for precisely fifteen
minutes. You know what a state I was in. I didn't even
have the presence of mind to offer her a drink. If I'd
known you'd seen her car, if I'd known what the
children had said to you, I'd——'

'You'd what?' She was smiling now, almost laughing.

But Leon wasn't. He was very serious indeed. 'I
wouldn't have wasted another week of my life. I'd have
come after you then and sorted you out.'

'Sorted me out? A fine way of putting it! Don't you
realise I've been under the impression all these weeks
that you were still into your affair with Heidi?'

He seemed shocked at that. 'For heaven's sake! You
don't think I'd—so *that's* why my African seduction
scene didn't come off!'

Suddenly they were arguing again! Cherry glared at
him indignantly, accusingly. 'So you had planned that
week-end! Right down to the last detail!'

'Of course I had. You'd been driving me crazy for
long enough, teasing me beyond endurance . . .'

'I did no such thing!'

He laughed at that, drawing her towards him.
'Darling Cherry, your very existence is a tease.' He
kissed her, he kissed her endlessly, passionately, but it
was he who broke it off. 'Darling, I had no idea, no

idea how you felt about me. I was trying to——' He sighed, shrugging. 'I suppose I was trying to rush things, to force your hand. You know, you're such a mysterious creature. When you're angry, your eyes spit blue flames at me. When you're happy or curious, that shows too. But I didn't know—well, the first time I kissed you, that time in the lift, you were furious, you wouldn't even speak to me for an hour afterwards! What was I supposed to make of you? I was so unsure of—of everything! All I knew was that I was in love with you, and it had hit me like a tidal wave. I knew from the start that I loved you, that day you barged into my office. And I fought against it. I actually wished you'd leave in the beginning. I didn't want to love again, I didn't want the emotional involve——'

'Hush, darling.' Cherry put her fingers against his lips, cuddling closer against him. She understood what he was saying, she understood it only too well.

'But you can't escape the inevitable,' he went on, seeming very happy to accept the inevitable. 'My grandmother told me that.'

'Your grandmother? What—what did she tell you, exactly?' She was alarmed again. 'Did she tell you—I mean, did she say anything about me?'

'Well, when I got back from Africa, it was she who told me how I felt about you—which was something I already knew! She asked me whether I'd told you, and I said no, that I couldn't because I had no idea how you felt.'

'She urged me to tell you. And when I did, finally, you ran away. Boy, did I give her some stick about that!'

'You horrible man! How can you treat an old lady like that? She didn't know about Heidi Reynolds, about all the complications! Er—what else did she say? The night I ran away, I mean?'

'She told me I didn't understand women.'

Cherry laughed her head off at that. 'Of course,' he

went on, 'what she really meant was that I don't understand Piscean women.'

'Of course.'

He was laughing now. 'She'd done your birth chart, you know. I'd guessed that was what she'd been up to. She wanted to talk to you about that, last Saturday.' His smile was wry. 'She talked to me instead. She'd compared your chart with mine and she went on at me about them, saying we were made for each other. As if I needed to be told ... it's all a lot of mumbo jumbo, and right now I have better things not to talk about.'

He lifted her face for his kiss, covering her mouth with his own, kissing her deeply, hungrily, until she was pressing herself tightly against him, moulding herself against the hardness of his body. 'Cherry ...' He murmured against her ear, his breathing deepening as she caressed him, planting tiny kisses on his neck, his throat. 'Let me hear you say it again. Tell me you love me and you'll marry me just as quickly as we can arrange it.'

She told him, but not in words. But she pulled away at length because in spite of what they were doing, she was desperately curious ...!

'Darling, what else did Grannie say—about our birth charts?'

'Oh, Cherry! Really! Come *here*!' Was she going to drive him mad daily, every day for the rest of his life?

'What else did she say?'

He was grinning, despairing over her, loving her, laughing with her. 'Oh, something about your Venus and my Mars.'

'And what does that mean?'

'*I* don't know! But she had a very wicked glint in her eyes as she told me how compatible they were ...' There was a wicked glint in his eyes, too, as he drew her into his arms again, his hands moving slowly towards the soft swell of her breasts. 'So I suggest we find out for ourselves, my darling ...'

*You're invited to accept 4 books and a surprise gift Free!*

# Acceptance Card

**Mail to: Harlequin Reader Service®**

In the U.S.
2504 West Southern Ave.
Tempe, AZ 85282

In Canada
P.O. Box 2800, Postal Station A
5170 Yonge Street
Willowdale, Ontario M2N 6J3

**YES!** Please send me 4 free Harlequin Presents® novels and my free surprise gift. Then send me 8 brand new novels every month as they come off the presses. Bill me at the low price of $1.75 each ($1.95 in Canada)—an 11% saving off the retail price. There are no shipping, handling or other hidden costs. There is no minimum number of books I must purchase. I can always return a shipment and cancel at any time. Even if I never buy another book from Harlequin, the 4 free novels and the surprise gift are mine to keep forever.

108 BPP-BPGE

| | |
|---|---|
| Name | (PLEASE PRINT) |

| | |
|---|---|
| Address | Apt. No. |

| | | |
|---|---|---|
| City | State/Prov. | Zip/Postal Code |

This offer is limited to one order per household and not valid to present subscribers. Price is subject to change.

ACP-SUB-1

# EYE OF THE STORM

## MAURA SEGER

A powerful
portrayal of
the events of
World War II in the
Pacific, *Eye of the Storm* is a riveting story of how love
triumphs over hatred. In this, the first of a three-book
chronicle, Army nurse Maggie Lawrence meets Marine
Sgt. Anthony Gargano. Despite military regulations
against fraternization, they resolve to face together
whatever lies ahead.... Author Maura Seger, also known
to her fans as Laurel Winslow, Sara Jennings, Anne
MacNeil and Jenny Bates, was named 1984's
Most Versatile Romance Author by *The Romantic Times*.

*You're invited to accept 4 books and a surprise gift Free!*

# Acceptance Card

**Mail to: Harlequin Reader Service®**

| In the U.S. | In Canada |
|---|---|
| 2504 West Southern Ave. | P.O. Box 2800, Postal Station A |
| Tempe, AZ 85282 | 5170 Yonge Street |
| | Willowdale, Ontario M2N 6J3 |

**YES!** Please send me 4 free Harlequin Romance® novels and my free surprise gift. Then send me 6 brand new novels every month as they come off the presses. Bill me at the low price of $1.65 each ($1.75 in Canada)—an 11% saving off the retail price. There are no shipping, handling or other hidden costs. There is no minimum number of books I must purchase. I can always return a shipment and cancel at any time. Even if I never buy another book from Harlequin, the 4 free novels and the surprise gift are mine to keep forever.

116 BPR-BPGE

Name _____ (PLEASE PRINT)

Address _____ Apt. No. _____

City _____ State/Prov. _____ Zip/Postal Code _____

This offer is limited to one order per household and not valid to present subscribers. Price is subject to change.

ACR-SUB-1